Chatham Square

www.cyberworldpublishing.com

Books By Olivia Stowe

Spirit of Christmas

Chatham Square

By the Howling

Retired With Prejudice

Fiddler's Rest

Chatham

Square

Olivia Stowe

Chapter One

"I should have brought a newspaper or a book or something."

Nearly unpacked, having already survived her first class at the Savannah College of Art and Design in the old Barnard School building across the square, and feeling the itch to get back to her dolls, Ginny had eschewed the thought of fixing her own breakfast of burned toast and weak coffee this morning and ventured out onto the square to William's Café at the corner at West Taylor.

The serious and mournful-looking young man two tables over had brought his book and hadn't looked up once since Ginny sat down. There were just the two of them on the outdoor patio of the café, which was not unusual for this time of day.

Ginny was intrigued that he was reading a book on textile art, which was what she was teaching at the college on an interim assignment while she determined what she thought of Savannah as a more permanent home. He was nice-looking enough. Clean cut and his hair nicely trimmed—something Ginny had seen little of in her class the previous afternoon. As scruffy as all of her students were—at least the ones who showed up half awake—Ginny wondered how they could turn out fine art work. But she had been assured that they did. And as the class progressed and when it was over and she walked down the hallways of the old school building, with its walls plastered with examples of their work, Ginny decided that maybe this was the right decision after all—at least for the interim.

It had been an eerie coincidence. She had barely come to the conclusion that she simply couldn't go on in Richmond, living in the Fan district and teaching the art of doll making at Virginia Commonwealth even for another month, when, on successive days, she'd received an offer to teach at SCAD for a term at least and notification that she had inherited her Aunt Marie's co-op apartment on one of Savannah's old squares. Ginny took it as an even clearer signal when she discovered that the building she'd be teaching in—Savannah's famous school of art and design being housed in old buildings all over the sleepy preeminent southern city—was right on the same square where her aunt's apartment was located. Chatham Square, one of the quietest, most picturesque, and charming of the squares mapped out for the original city plan.

The bequest had been a curious one. Ginny had known her aunt only through a series of letters exchanged over the years without the knowledge of Ginny's mother, Marie's sister. There had been some sort of falling out between the two sisters. But Marie had persisted in sending letters to Ginny on the sly until Ginny broke down and realized that she looked forward to the chat and worldly advice from the woman and opened up to her in writing—in ways that she didn't open up even to her mother.

Marie had hidden her illness from Ginny over the past year—being more focused on Ginny's own activities—only hinting at her condition by repeatedly suggesting that it would be nice if Ginny came down to Savannah to visit her sooner rather than later. In hindsight, considering what happened not long before Marie died, Ginny came to believe that she had been insensitive and self-centered in her relationship with her aunt. She hadn't come—at least before Marie unexpectedly did die.

It wasn't because of where Ginny lived or what she taught that had become oppressive to her. It was because of Lenny. Lenny had shared Richmond with her. Wherever she turned, a memory slipped back in of what she and Lenny had done here or there. What Lenny had said. How he had smiled at her—that "forever" smile. That smile that now seemed so false and curdled her blood—blood that had run hot for Lenny. All too briefly, but all too painful now. Lenny had been her first love. She was told she'd get over it, but she didn't think that was possible.

Her Aunt Marie hadn't told her to just get over it; she had counseled that Ginny should get away—change her environment and her activity patterns and look for new, surer footing. And then, while to two were discussing plans for a visit

9

by Ginny, Aunt Marie had died—and left Ginny her co-op apartment in Savannah, on Chatham Square, in what was one of the first cities in the New World to be designed for urban livability on paper before foundations were laid and paths cleared for roads.

Arriving in Savannah, Ginny had been pleasantly surprised. It was different from Richmond—sleepier, more southern, if it was possible to be more southern than Richmond. She had to admit, however, that Richmond was becoming northernized and urbanized at a fast pace—much faster a pace than she was seeing in Savannah. But in those differences, there also were similarities that made the transition easier for her. Old Savannah was of much the same cloth as the Fan district of Richmond where she had lived. And the art school. Well, creative students are a blessing no matter where they are found. And her work and her students truly were blessings for Ginny. She had no idea how she would have survived the loss of Lenny otherwise.

Whenever Ginny felt hurt or depressed, there were always her dolls. She could always begin making another doll. She could put all of her expression in her art.

What surprised her, though, were the people. Whenever she said she was moving down to Savannah, the first thing she would hear about was the graciousness and friendliness of the people of Savannah—and then they would mention the city's squares and how restful and serene they were.

But thus far Ginny hadn't seen any of the friendliness, except perhaps glimmers—no, to be fair, more than glimmers—

of it at the college. She was trying to be fair. She hadn't been here long enough to make sweeping judgments. But thus far graciousness and friendliness weren't the first traits that came to mind concerning the people of Chatham Square—from the bag lady haunting the otherwise magical park in the square, taking up the best bench and humming her songs and rocking back and forth and not even looking up when greeted, to the man in one of the two hunkering Greek Revival piles glowering at each other across the square, one on the west and the other on the east, who gave nothing more than a curt, "Yes, it is," when Ginny had passed him the previous morning en route to the college and remarked on the beautiful morning.

Ginny had already fallen into gritting her teeth when coming back to her new home, a very nice two-bedroom, second-floor apartment with large, high-ceilinged rooms and large windows fronting the square on one side and a charming walled stone patio in the back that was shared by all. The apartment was one of several in a row of old townhouses lining the southern side of the square that one would take for separate single-family dwellings in passing. The co-op idea had sounded inviting when Ginny had been told of the apartment—but she already was learning the downside of that.

The first-floor apartment in her section of the townhouses was owned by a crotchety old man who Ginny had, thus far, principally experienced by the view of his bent back and a broad rear as he flounced back into his apartment from their shared foyer and slammed his door. Ginny had found several things that needed immediate attention when she had moved in—a leak in the roof tiles, plumbing that banged and balked, and a broken step on the stairs down to the street from the entry. And she had quickly learned that in a co-op arrangement, these had to be commonly addressed. But so far, Mr. Richards, on the first floor, snapped and retreated at any mention of a common solution to the problems—and the couple who owned the third floor apartment apparently weren't even in residence. There was a smaller apartment in the English basement, but Ginny saw as she was moving in that it had a foreclosure sign on the door that dated back into the previous year.

And here, as cheery and inviting as William's café had looked when she passed it on the way home from the college the previous afternoon, it certainly wasn't lifting her spirits now, despite the delicious, chicory-smelling coffee and the flakey croissants she found there. And she knew exactly why. The people here were pulling her down. There were only two of them besides Ginny at the outdoor café this morning—the young man who had his nose in the book and who was spoiling his handsome features with a perpetual frown and the waiter, who was even more glum than the book reader was. It wasn't that he was inattentive; it was that he seemed to be miles and miles away.

And at this moment, Ginny wasn't at all sure she had solved anything by moving miles and miles away herself—putting distance between herself and the memory of Lenny.

She was deep enough in thought going back to her apartment that she forgot about the broken step and almost tripped. Mr. Richards was standing inside his door when she entered the foyer—he always seemed to be there to see her come in even though he didn't want to talk to her when she did.

"I almost tripped on the stair again, Mr. Richards. We really must do something about that. And about the roof too—they say we're expecting some heavy rains next week."

"Do what you want about it, young lady. I don't have money for such as that. Your aunt, Marie, she never—"

"I'm sure she didn't, Mr. Richards. That's why—"

"Don't need any of your sass, either, young lady. Savannah girls don't—"

"Oh, all right. I'll call around for someone to start fixing them," Ginny said, exasperated and feeling the familiar dread of irritation and aloneness clutching at her. Richards said nothing—until Ginny had reached the fourth stair and couldn't resist saying over her shoulder, "I'll get the work done. But it's a co-op. I'll send you a bill for a third of the cost."

"I didn't OK any billing," he muttered. "And there's the basement apartment too. It's not my fault that unit's in foreclosure. I'm not liable for any more than a fourth of anything on this hall."

Ginny heard Richards's door slam right before she slammed hers. She felt foolish. He was just a grouchy old man. He probably felt as alone as she did. There was no evidence there was a Mrs. Richards, but the glimpses that Ginny had gotten of the living room of that unit around Mr. Richards's retreating back showed definite signs of a woman's taste and touch.

Ginny went into the second bedroom that she was using as a workroom and sat down to work on the latest doll she was making. Ginny didn't make dolls for play; she made elaborate historical period dolls as art objects. Each one cost hundreds of dollars to make and hundreds more than that to own. It was her art, and she made good money at it. She also was good enough at it that she was widely sought as an art instructor and gallery exhibitor.

She was having trouble concentrating on the doll she was working on today, though. The isolation at the café and this little set-to with Mr. Richards had put her out of sorts. No, she realized, she already had been out of sorts. Now she was downright despondent. This was how she had felt when she had left Richmond. Her first two weeks in Savannah had been more uplifting, but now she was sinking fast back into what she knew would become clinical depression if she didn't do something about it.

The letter was there on her work table. She'd read it a thousand times already. She reached out to take it up again, but then she jerked her hand back. She wouldn't do it. She wouldn't let herself wallow in her grief and misfortunate—and her shame.

She had to get out of the house—into the sunshine or the shade or a pretty garden. It didn't matter what. She just needed to try to do something she wasn't now doing to lift her spirits.

Maybe if she made a lunch she could take out into the park in the square. A picnic. She decided it was worth a try.

She'd take the doll and do some fancy embroidery on the gown it was wearing—or maybe fashion something regal to pin into the doll's elaborate white powdered coiffure.

The bag lady was occupying the bench with the best mix of sunlight and shade when Ginny entered the park. This was no surprise, of course, but the woman didn't make any gesture of moving enough to one side for Ginny to sit there too. So Ginny sat on a bench facing the woman.

Fed by a cry for human contact deep inside her, Ginny took half of the sandwich she had made and reached out over the pathway that separated the two women. "I've found my eyes were bigger than my stomach. I can't eat all of this sandwich I just made. Would you like to have half?"

The woman stopped humming and rocking and looked up at the proffered sandwich and then into Ginny's eyes. If Ginny had expected to receive some spark of contact, she was disappointed, because there was nothing but the look of indifference in the woman's eyes. Ginny couldn't determine her age. She could have been anywhere between fifty and seventy. She wasn't dirty, but there was an air of unkemptness and "I don't care" about her, which Ginny thought was a shame, because the woman had a face that once must have been strikingly beautiful. There was no way of telling whether she was malnourished or obese, because she had wrapped herself in many layers of clothing. She no doubt was wearing everything she owned, Ginny thought.

The woman was surrounded by bits and pieces of what looked like cast-off and completely useless mismatched material. She held a pair of scissors, and the way she was wielding them as she cut away at the material scraps made Ginny wary.

Ginny heard the woman give a grunt, and when she looked up, she saw the woman shrug and gesture toward a piece of cardboard sitting on the bench beside her. Ginny shuffled over to the other side of the path and put the half of sandwich down on the cardboard and quickly retreated to her own bench, her eyes all the time on the flashing scissors.

Almost immediately a flock of birds descended on the pathway in front the old woman, and Ginny watched in irritation and surprise as the woman took up the sandwich and pinched away at it, tossing bits and pieces of the bread and meat to the dancing birds as she did so.

Of course Ginny felt insulted—and put in her place. She had meant it as a gesture of introduction, of friendship, not of pity and smug charity. But it had been taken wrong. She felt she had been done a wrong herself, but, equally, she wondered if it had been she who had gone beyond the bounds.

She just didn't know anymore. Ever since she had received that letter—that letter from Lenny—she had been off kilter. Her whole world had gone awry and she had begun to question everything she did—why she did it. Were her motives good or self-centered?

Ginny was still struggling with this while she busied herself with what she brought to work on and tried not to look at the old woman, who had gone back to her mad stabbing at the scraps of material as the birds lost interest for the moment and flew back up into the trees overhead.

It was while Ginny was trying to avoid a confrontation that she noticed a little girl standing at the arm of her bench. She was a little black girl of seven or eight in a loose-fitting cotton dress, white—or once white—with tiny lilacs on it, and with tightly pulled cornrow pigtails.

"Hello there. How are you?" Ginny said with a smile, trying to cover up the snub she'd just received and show that she was "the nice one."

"Fine."

Ginny recognized her as the daughter of a woman who lived in the basement apartment of the section of the co-op building just to the west of hers. The woman had been recommended to her as a cleaning lady by the realty company that had watched over her apartment while the inheritance papers went through and Ginny was able to take possession. The woman apparently cleaned several of the co-op apartments on the square and was a housemaid for the Armstrong Inn that also occupied a portion of the square. There was no sign of a father that Ginny had seen as yet.

"Would you like to have a cookie? I have more here than I can eat."

"No ma'am. Can't. My mamma says I can't."

Yet another rebuff. But at least this time it was for a sensible parental protection reason. Ginny could see that the little girl very much would like to have one of the cookies and that there wouldn't be any questions of the birds getting any of it if she had it.

"It's still in the package, honey. Sealed. I haven't opened it. So, why don't you just take it home with you and give it to your mother and ask her if it would be all right for you to eat it?"

"Yes, ma'am. Thank you ma'am."

Ginny saw signs of a slight curtsy as an obviously pleased little girl reached out a small, thin hand and delicately took the cookie package. Ginny was already on edge from earlier in the day and from the encounter she'd just had with the woman who was still sitting across the path now—and now showing more interest in Ginny and the little girl than she had shown to just Ginny, and Ginny felt herself trembling—on the point of both tears and a nervous giggle. She willed the little girl to turn and run off home, but the girl just stood there and looked at her, a mixed smile and quizzical look on her face.

"What is it, dear? Do you want something else?" Ginny asked. She felt the words clutch at her throat, though. She felt overwhelmed and full of regret for having come to the park.

"Is that a doll?"

"Yes, it's a doll," Ginny said, the tension beginning to drain from her now. She was returning to sure footing.

"What's wrong with it?"

"Nothing's wrong with it. I'm still making it. I make dolls. See," Ginny said, as she lifted the doll. "It's a queen doll."

"Why is the queen so sad?"

It was a simple question, but it shot through to Ginny's very being like a bolt of lightning. She looked at the face of the doll, and indeed, it did look very sad indeed. How could this have happened? This wasn't how she made her dolls. How could she have painted a sad face on the doll and not have known she was doing it?

"She's a queen who led a very sad life, dear." It was the best answer she could come up with on the spur of the moment. And that it was true quite probably wouldn't be either here or there in the view of a child. It did seem to satisfy the little girl, though.

"Do you make happy dolls too? I like happy dolls."

Ginny started to answer, but both she and the little girl looked away, toward the line of row houses on the south side of the square as they heard a woman calling. It was the little girl's mother. With a little apologetic smile, the girl turned and limped away.

It was then that Ginny noticed that the girl's legs were malformed—well, at least that one of them was. It was turned outward so that the girl's right foot was pointed at an outward angle rather than straight. She was trying to run to her mother, but she couldn't manage more than an awkward lope and constantly had to correct her movement to remain in some semblance of a straight line.

"Yes, of course I make happy dolls," Ginny murmured as she watched the little girl struggle down the park pathway, her voice choked by a tear that had appeared.

Ginny tore her gaze away from the departing figure of the little girl and looked across the pathway at the woman on the other bench—who now was looking at her sharply.

Was that a judgmental stare? A dare for Ginny to show some emotion, some misplaced sense of pity and charity?

Ginny didn't wait around to find out. She gathered up her doll and what was left of her ruined lunch and hurried across the park in the wake of the little girl and back into her apartment.

She stopped inside the closed door of her apartment, her back plastered to the strong wood separating her from the world, to catch her breath. When she could breathe again, she headed straight for her workroom and scanned the shelves to examine her dolls—the pieces of work in various stages of completion—knowing now what she would find, what she didn't want to see. Sad faces. Every face she had painted on every oblong object of porcelain or wood that represented a doll face in preparation bore a sad expression. These were all faces she's painted since receiving the letter from Lenny.

She sank into the chair at her work table and took up the letter—the letter from Lenny—the last letter from Lenny. The letter Lenny had written her from his deployment in Iraq, where his National Guard unit had been sent when he was jerked up from his job as a graphics art assistant professor at VCU in Richmond and was marched off to war.

Faithfully for ten months Ginny had received a letter from him dated on Sunday. All on Sunday, except for the last one, dated on a Saturday.

Ginny began to read the letter, this one had been impersonally typed, whereas all of the rest had been written in his hand, and this one signed Leonard, rather than Lenny—the letter in form screaming to her what was to be found inside even before she'd read it. She didn't really have to look at the words now—they were burned in her memory—but she read them again anyway.

Ginny:

I had been told that distancing would clear one's thoughts, but I never believed that was true. Until now. We never really had a chance, you know. We were thrown together by others in Richmond and just went along with what everyone else wanted. At least I did. I've met someone else here in Iraq. She's a field doctor and is doing something important with her life. She is saving lives out here. And being with her now has made me realize that I never did really see you clearly. I hadn't realized how much of everything was for you and because you wanted it. I didn't realize that I was losing me and how little room there was in your life for me. Or anyone else. It's perhaps fortunate for us both that I came to Iraq, because . . .

Ginny couldn't read any more. She often didn't even get this far in the letter. There wasn't much more in the letter anyway—certainly nothing comforting.

She let the letter drop back on the worktable and buried her face in her folded arms and let the tears of frustration and loneliness out that had been begging for release all day.

Chapter Two

"Is that a doll you're working on?"

It was the most personal thing the waiter at William's Café had said to her in three visits.

Ginny looked up, smiled at him, and said "Yes. It's supposed to be Marie Antoinette. I'm working on the embroidering of the dress now."

"It's gorgeous. I love the fabric; it's fab," he said as he poured the coffee into her cup. The way he said it made her look up sharply. At first she thought maybe he was mocking her, but it now looked more likely that he wasn't. It was something in the way he held his body—a thin, wispy sort of body, or maybe the angle of his wrist when he poured the coffee and then flipped it up as he drew the pot away. Funny that she hadn't noticed this before. He was quite good looking in a sultry way—what they called a quadroon in the far south, Ginny thought—a portion of both Caucasian and black, taking all of the best-looking traits of each. But he was more beautiful than handsome. And now that Ginny was observing him

23

closely, it was evident he had traces of makeup on his face—lipstick even.

But he still looked so sad.

It didn't matter to Ginny, of course, what his preferences were. She was just surprised that she had been so unobservant until now. Perhaps it hadn't been just him who had been disengaged when she was in here before. Maybe how he had related had something to do with her own observable persona. Obviously Lenny would say that it did—that it was her more than the waiter who was responsible for the distancing.

Ginny decided to work on that—not just with the waiter, but with others too.

"Yes, the material is authentic. She reputably actually wore a gown in this material. I got it from Paris. I'll have to repaint her face, though, I think. She's too sad."

"Well, Marie Antoinette had every right to be sad faced, don't you think?" he answered. He was giving her a little smile now. Just as she was noticing him for the first time, he was noticing her. And she got the impression that he discerned she needed a little smile from someone—which, of course, she did.

Ginny decided that he needed a smile back, so she gave him one, and she was pleased to see that it obviously pleased him.

"Yes, but this dress is for her 'let's pretend' court days, when she was putting on her best face. So, perhaps I should let her have her way."

"I'm sure she would appreciate that. Marie Antoinette was very particular about her public persona," he answered.

And for some reason, Ginny got the impression that this discussion was so much more meaningful for the waiter than for her.

"You've now been here for breakfast three of the past five days," he went on to say. "I probably should be referring to you by name so everyone knows you're a preferred customer."

Ginny laughed. "I'm Ginny Standler. I live over there in the co-ops on the south side of the square. I teach at SCAD."

"Standler? But you look familiar. You wouldn't, by any chance, be related to Marie Purcell. She was a good customer and lived over there too."

"Yes, she was my aunt. I inherited her apartment."

"She was a nice lady. She preferred the French toast. It really is better here than the croissants are."

"I'll remember that. And you? You must be William, I suppose?"

He gave her a quizzical look at that.

"William, as in William's Café? You're the only one I've seen working here, so I assume you are the owner."

"No, alas," he said with a laugh. "I'm only the chief flunkey. The William stands for William Pitt. That's who this square is named for. He was the Earl of Chatham."

And then, as Ginny's chuckle subsided, he said, "I'm Tony."

And after he turned to go back inside, he turned again and gave Ginny a wink and said, "Tony. Short for Antoinette."

Ginny left the café in a better mood than she'd been in for days. She still wondered what in Tony's life made him sad, but she was happy that they both had lifted each other's spirits today. She supposed that there might be a lot in the life of such a young man that would be challenging—especially for someone of mixed parentage and even here in Savannah, which seemed so laid back and devil may care. But she didn't care what others might think. Tony's was the first given name she'd collected in Savannah. She considered that a great victory for a morning's effort.

She decided to treat herself and drop in at the bookstore across the square from the café. She wanted to know what art books they had—what they might have to add to her fund of knowledge in her doll making. She figured they would have a good collection, being in the center of the footprint left by the scattered buildings of the arts and design college.

To get there, she had to walk by the house of that gruff man who lived in the large, foreboding Greek Revival house on the west side of the square. And she could see as she approached the house that she wasn't going to avoid another probable snub, because he was coming off his porch as she was crossing the street.

"You've been talking with the old woman out in the park," he said, making it sound like an accusation.

"Excuse me?" He had caught her completely by surprise. She hadn't expected him to say anything to her—and she was shocked he was commenting on the previous day's fiasco in the park. That was the only time she'd come anywhere close to the bag lady on the bench. Was he spying?

"You know, she shouldn't be out there all day like that. It scares people off—and she hogs the best bench. I've complained to the authorities, but they say there's nothing they can do unless she assaults someone. She didn't assault you, did she?"

"No," Ginny answered, still in shock—but she reddened as the image of flashing scissors ran through her mind, and she had to agree that it was irritating that the woman seemed to have taken permanent claim to the best bench in the square. "No, we didn't say hardly anything at all to each other. I'm sure she's harmless."

"She's poison. I'd stay away from her, if I were you."

And then there was no more to be said, as he'd turned and stomped back up onto his porch and into his house.

Ginny was still shaking her head over that, when she descended the short flight of stairs at the corner to enter the Pitt Bookstore, which occupied an English basement at one of the square's corners. She was surprised as her eyes adjusted to the dim light to see the young book reader from the café the other morning sitting behind a desk near the entrance.

"Oh, hello there," she said. "I'm Ginny Standler. I live just there in the apartment block on the south side of the square." She paused, waiting—in vain—for a return introduction that didn't come. "I think I saw you at the café across the square the other day."

"Yes, may I help you with something?"

"Your art books. Especially anything you might have on art dolls."

"Oh?" Was it her imagination, or did his voice sound slightly warmer?

"Yes, please. I make art dolls, and I thought perhaps—"

"Oh," he said as he rose—and the "Oh" sounded warmer yet. "Yes, we have quite a good collection. Back here, please. It's not at the front of the shop—that's pretty much taken up with copies of *Midnight in the Garden of Good and Evil* and paraphernalia on that—our bread and butter, you understand. The Mercer house and the setting for that murder trial and movie are just one square over in Monterey Square, you'll understand. It pays the rent." He sounded downright apologetic about that.

"How interesting," Ginny said—as if it was the first time she'd heard about the premier local legend.

"I'd be interested in all of your art books on textiles, in fact. I'm teaching over at SCAD in the old Barnard School building on the other side of square."

"Oh, in that case, let me go find a stool. You'll probably want to spend some time back in that corner over there . . . Miss. Standler . . . and would you like a cup of tea? I have a kettle on perpetual boil back in the back."

"It's Ginny, and yes, thank you. I'd love a cup, Mr. . . ."

"Tom. Tom Thornton. I'm Tom."

Ginny was fairly skipping, having collected two first names among the locals, when she crossed the street some hours later to start down the southern side of the square—only to be stopped up cold, at the sight of a crumpled Mr. Richards at the foot of the stairs up to their shared entryway.

"Mr. Richards," she exclaimed as she bent down. "What's the matter?"

"Damned step. Should have been fixed a long time ago."

"Here, let me help you up and into your apartment. And then let's have a look at that."

"No need to fuss. I can—"

But clearly he couldn't, as he exhibited by wincing and collapsing again when he tried to stand.

Ginny helped him up to his apartment and into an overstuffed chair just inside the door from the foyer into his living room. She surveyed the damage and decided it was probably just a bad sprain.

"That will need to be washed off and bandaged, though—tightly, so that we can keep the swelling down."

She turned and headed toward the kitchen. She had her hand on the handle of the closed door, though, when Richards called out, almost in panic, "No not that door. The kitchen's over there. That room's closed."

It was only then that Ginny noticed that Mr. Richard's apartment wasn't a match in floor plan to her own. She had assumed it would be, but these were old existing buildings they had renovated, originally built for individual residences, and obviously they'd attempted to stay with original walls and spaces as much as possible.

"Oh, sorry," she said—while wondering why that was a room not to go into. The apartment wasn't any larger than hers in square footage, it seemed. The apartments were commodious, but not so much so that there was room to toss away.

But getting him cleaned up and settled took most of the next half hour and took her thoughts off the forbidden room as well. When she was finished and had his leg bandaged and propped up on a footstool, she had to face the inevitable. "Do you have anyone . . . ? I see there are photographs of you around with a woman."

"No, that was my wife, Anne. She . . . died a few years ago. There's no one. But—"

"Then I'll be back with some supper for you in a couple of hours, of course. We'll see what the night does for that ankle of yours. And then we'll see what needs to be done tomorrow."

"I couldn't possibly—"

"It's much too late to do anything about it now. I don't have a car yet, and unless you do—"

"Uh, no I don't."

"And unless you want to spring for an ambulance over a twisted ankle."

He didn't have to answer that one.

"Well, don't go out of your way on food or anything or worry about hitting it right at six, Miss. . . ."

"It's Ginny. We're neighbors. That's what neighbors do for each other."

"Uh . . . thanks . . . , Ginny. I'm Arnold. Most folks call me Arnie. And, Ginny . . ."

"Yes?"

30

"Thanks. Thanks for your help. I'll call the services tomorrow—for the step . . . and the roof . . . and the plumbing."

"Thanks, but I've already called."

"And I'll be happy to split the cost with you—until we can track down the owners of the other two apartments."

"Thanks, Arnie. That would be very nice."

In all of that, Ginny realized she hadn't gotten any lunch yet—and she doubted she'd make it until supper. And there was a bit more embroidery she wanted to do on the Marie Antoinette doll. But there was something she wanted to do first. She took the doll to the workroom and found the paint thinner and wiped the face off the doll. She thought Marie deserved a happy face. This would be the queen in her earlier days.

One look out a front window told Ginny the park was gorgeous under dappled sunshine—and deserted, so she decided to fix a sandwich and work on the doll out in the square.

By the time she got everything together and was crossing the road into the park, Ginny saw that two young boys had come into the park and were throwing a Frisbee back and forth between them. The little girl from the previous day was sitting in the grass not far from them and watching their every movement.

When Ginny reached the benches at the center of the square, fully intending to take the one the bag lady usually occupied, she found that she just couldn't do it. So, she made do with the one she'd sat on the previous day.

31

And a good thing she had, too, as she'd barely gotten settled when the woman appeared and claimed "her" bench. They said nothing to each other—barely even looked at each other—as the bag lady distributed her bits and pieces of material in a pattern about her the order of which only she could fathom and Ginny unwrapped the sandwich she'd brought.

Several minutes of silence followed. But nothing lasts forever.

"Are you going to eat all of that?"

"No, I suppose not," Ginny answered reflexively, in shock that the woman had actually spoken to her. The woman's voice was low and rich—and surprisingly refined. "Would you like to have half?" Ginny ventured.

"Yes, if you can spare it, thank you. I didn't realize I was hungry until I sat down."

Ginny handed over half her sandwich, half expecting the birds to be getting a feast, but, though the birds showed up, this time the sandwich wasn't for the birds. Each of the women munched on her half, both obviously enjoying it.

"Her name's Samantha," the woman said as she finished her half and was licking her fingers and murmuring apologies to the disappointed flock of birds at her feet. "Tomorrow, my pets. I promise."

"Excuse me, what did you say?"

"The birds. I was apologizing to the birds. They expect me to feed them. I think of them now as the children I never had. And their song gives me company, so I feed them when I can."

"That's nice. But, no, I mean you said something about Samantha."

"The girl. The girl at your elbow. Her name's Samantha. And I think she likes you."

Ginny turned, startled, to find that the little girl with the crippled leg was, indeed, standing at her elbow, right where she stood the day before.

"I'm sorry, honey. I don't have any cookies today. If I'd known—"

"That's OK, thanks. I still have half of the one from yesterday. My mamma said I could eat it since it was still in its package. Did you bring a doll today?"

"Yes, indeed I did. Come, sit by me. I'll let you do a stitch or two, if you like. And then we can say you helped make this doll."

Samantha came around to the front of the bench and sat down primly, fanning the skirt of her cotton dress out like she was posing at a cotillion. "Did you bring a happy doll today?"

"We can make it a happy doll if you would like to come to my workshop some day," Ginny answered. She held the doll out for the little girl to see. "Look at her face. She isn't sad anymore. She isn't anything now. But we can make her however we want her."

"We can make her well?"

"Yes, of course—if she gets sick." Ginny looked into the face of Samantha then and saw that the little girl was watching the two boys playing Frisbee. Ginny was at a loss for words, and her heart ached for the little girl.

"My daddy's going to bring home money so they can make my leg well again," Samantha said in a steady, clear voice. "He took his trumpet and went to a place called Naw Leans, where he said he could make a pile of money. He's going to bring it all home and then I'm going to the hospital for a bit and then I'm going to get me a bicycle—all my own. And when I gits older, I'm goin' to go work in that hospital. I'se gonna become a doctor that straightens legs. I told my mamma that, and she told me I could do just whatever I wanted to do when I growed up."

"That's nice, honey. I'm glad to hear that."

Ginny had trouble getting that sentence out and she couldn't speak for the next couple of minutes, but she didn't need to. Samantha chattered on about her school work and her mother and father and how she liked one of the boys over there throwing a Frisbee, but not the other, because he made fun of the way she walked. And then she just sort of wound down and decided it was time for her to go see what her mother was doing. "She said she was gonna bake a cake today. For the church bazaar."

All the time, the lady on the other bench continued humming and rocking, and arranging and rearranging the bits of material gathered around her. At least she wasn't armed with any scissors today.

When Samantha was gone Ginny gathered up her materials, rose from the bench, and turned to walk back across the street to her apartment.

"I hear your name is Ginny. That you're Marie Purcell's niece."

"Yes, yes, I am," Ginny said in surprise, as she turned toward the woman on the other bench.

"I liked Marie. She was a fine woman. She helped me feed the birds. My name is Rose."

"Hello, Rose, I'm pleased to meet you."

"And I'm pleased to make your acquaintance as well. Would you like to help me feed the birds tomorrow?"

"Yes, I think I would. Thanks for asking, Rose."

"Remember to bring bread for them. They prefer whole wheat."

Ginny stifled a giggle as she turned and walked toward her building.

Chapter Three

"You haven't asked me about the closed room."

"No I haven't," Ginny answered. "There, the ankles all wrapped, and it looks quite a bit better this evening than it did earlier today. For some reason Aunt Marie had a pair of crutches back in her storage room—I didn't ever know of her needing them—and I think you can probably get around well enough on these tonight. And maybe you won't need to go to the doctor's after all. I went down to the bookstore, though, and Tom Thornton down there says he can drive you someplace tomorrow if you need to go."

"Thanks, Ginny," Arnie Richards said. "That was beyond the call of duty. That Tom Thornton's a presentable lad, isn't he?"

Ginny's blush revealed that she did, indeed, think that Tom Thornton was a presentable lad.

"Would you like some more of the casserole?"

"No thanks. It was delicious. But I don't usually eat that fancy."

There was a moment of silence as Ginny cleared away the plate and silverware.

"You haven't asked me about the closed room."

"No . . . no, I haven't."

"If you'd like to hear about it, I think I'd like to tell you. I'd like to tell someone. It's been so lonely here since your Aunt Marie died. We used to talk. She knew my Anne. It was comforting to talk with someone who had known her. It was like she was still here. But now there's no one."

"I'm sorry, Arnie. Certainly, if you'd like to tell me anything, I'd be happy to hear it. I haven't had anyone to talk with for some time myself."

"Well, it starts in Kenya forty years ago. Can you hold with me that far back?"

"Maybe I should sit down, then," Ginny said. And the two laughed a comfortable laugh as she did so.

"Anne was British. And I was an adventurer. We met in Cairo and married in Jerusalem, and then we settled in Kenya, where we raised coffee."

"My, that sounds romantic."

"Yes, yes, it was. But then I strayed. I'm sorry, maybe you don't want to hear this part. After I'd stopped and tried to make it up to her, Marie said she was OK with it, but maybe you—"

"No, no, that's fine, Arnie. I'm a big girl. I've probably heard it all."

"And maybe done some of it too," Arnie said, then he looked embarrassed.

"No, unfortunately not nearly as much of it as I would have liked," Ginny responded. They both laughed at that, albeit not quite as comfortably as they had before—but Ginny knew this was new ground, that they were going deeper into whatever relationship there was to be between them and had actually taken a step up in trust. "But, please, go on," she said.

"Well, Anne said she forgave me. But I don't think she ever did. It wasn't the same after that—at least except for that time while she was ill."

"She was ill?"

"Yes, that was when we'd been married for a good twenty-five years, though. We worked hard, and we built that coffee business up until we had three plantations and were living high on the hog. We were in London on a 'just because' trip when she found out—when Anne found she had cancer."

"Oh. I'm sorry, so she died from—?"

"No she didn't. She fought it, tooth and nail—we both fought it. And she came out on the other side cancer free. But it broke us. All of the medical bills just took nearly everything, all three plantations. I managed to get a job with an American importer, though, and we settled here. Had enough money to buy this place when they were doing the renovations. Bought it with cash on the barrelhead. Which is a good thing, because I have no idea how we would have lived after I retired if we had to pay rent or a mortgage. But we were happy. Or so I thought."

Arnie went silent at that point, and Ginny didn't prompt him. She figured he'd start up again or think better of it and say no more. But either way, it was OK with her. Still, she didn't

38

have the foggiest notion what this had to do with the closed room.

"It was three years ago. Three years ago last April 14th. At two in the afternoon."

His voice was sounding tense now, and Ginny's mind was beginning to fantasize. Had he killed her? Was she still there, in that room? Surely not, if he said he'd talked with Aunt Marie about it. Aunt Marie wouldn't have stayed silent for something like that. Would she? Ginny had to admit that she didn't really know her Aunt Marie at all. And she felt a pang of guilt in realizing that Aunt Marie had tried—it was Ginny herself who hadn't committed to more than the exchange of letters.

"There, in that room."

Ginny was trembling, preparing herself to spring from the sofa and run for the door. Surely in Arnie's present state he couldn't get there before she could.

"She did it to herself. I thought we were happy. That all had been forgiven. That it was clear sailing from here."

A few moments of silence.

"Are you saying that your wife . . . that Anne . . . took her own life?"

"There, in that room. Pills. She must have collected sleeping pills for some time to have enough to do the job. On the chaise lounge in there. She liked to nap in that room. She called it her sanctuary. I never thought of that. Her sanctuary . . . from me, I guess. And I never had a clue."

"And the room has been closed?"

"From the moment they took her out of there. I could see how it was from the door. I didn't go in there. After then, after they took her out, I just closed the door and never opened it again."

"Oh, I'm so sorry. But maybe—"

"We were a handsome couple. In Kenya. Everyone said so. There's an album. Would you like to see—?"

"Yes, that would be nice."

"Damn."

"Excuse me? What?"

"The album. It's in that room."

"Well, then that's OK."

"No, no. I'd really like you to see the photos. I think I'd like to see them again myself. Now. You could go in there and get them. I've been a rather foolish old man, I guess. It's just a room."

"I don't really want to bother."

"No, please. I know right where the albums are. They're stacked on the mantle. There's a fireplace in there. That's why Anne wanted us to buy this place. There are fireplaces. She was pleased that her room, her sanctuary, would have a fireplace."

"If it's OK, then."

"Yes, please. It's time to give all that up. When my ankle's better, maybe I'll go in there too. Maybe. But, please, go on in and bring back the albums on the mantle."

Hesitatingly, Ginny rose from the sofa and went to the door of the room. She released her breath as she stood at the door, her hand on the handle, realizing that she had been holding her breath in as Arnie had zeroed in on the significance of that closed door. "It's just a room," she told herself as she turned the handle.

And indeed it was just a room. But obviously a woman's personal room, overflowing with memories of a full, rich life. Ginny tried not to even look at the chaise lounge as she passed it. She had expected cobwebs and layers of dust, but it wasn't really that bad. These old houses had good insulation. She saw that there was a short stack of photo albums on the mantle, just as Arnie said there would be.

But there also was a folded sheet of stationery that fluttered to the carpet as she moved the albums. She stooped and picked it up and instinctively looked at it. And then all of the armies of the world could not have stopped her from reading the letter.

My Dearest Arnie:

When you read this, I will be gone. I have tried to be gone for weeks now; the pain is here. It's back, and I find that enduring it is unbearable. And so I knew I had to be strong if only for a brief moment. Strong for both of us. I know we can't go through this again. Just as I know you would do it all over again. But we just can't. We no longer have the means. And I no longer have the strength. That has all drained away from the first time. And I'm so sorry for that. So sorry for this cancer in my body. So sorry that I couldn't have been the perfect wife you deserve. Please don't be mad that I have not told you and did not give you a proper good-bye. I am not as strong as I would like to be. If I don't do it this way, I'm afraid I won't do it at all. Please know that I love and have always loved . . .

At that point all of the armies of the world could not have forced Ginny to continue.

She didn't know how long she stood there, holding that letter, trying to compose herself. But she was brought back to reality by the questioning call from the other room.

"Ginny. Can't you find them? I'm sure they're—"

But he stopped, seeing the expression on Ginny's face, as she stood in the doorway to the forbidden room, letter in hand.

"You must read this, Arnie. I think you have suffered from a misconception for far too long."

Chapter Four

"And you didn't find that scary and awkward?"

"Maybe just a little bit. But after the shock was over, I felt really good about it. You should have seen Arnie after it had sunk in, Tom. And I think he lost a good ten years of care. He still claimed to be mad at her—he still said he'd have wanted them to fight it and that he'd have managed it some way. But it obviously was such a relief to him that it wasn't his guilt that had pushed her over the edge."

"His guilt? Uh, thanks, Tony, I would like a coffee refill, please."

Ginny and Tom were sitting—together—at an outside table at William's Café. Ginny had arrived first and then Tom, who had asked her if she cared if he joined her. He was still looking a little down in the mouth, but Ginny didn't care. Someone had asked to join her at her table. And not just anybody. Tom Thornton had asked if he could join her.

"Oh, he just always felt that it was something he'd done or not done that had made her do it. It's really not usually something someone resorts to unless they want to punish someone they're leaving behind. But in Anne's case, I think I can understand it all. And I think Arnie would have come to understand it a lot sooner. It was really unfortunate that he never went in the room. The letter was right there on the mantle, addressed to him. He would have known right away that, in Anne's mind, she was doing it for him and not to him. And who's to say she was wrong? She'd already been through all that pain and suffering the first time around. Who's to say she wasn't right in believing that living wasn't worth going through it all again, money to cover it or otherwise?"

"You were good to be there with him in the first place—and then to stick around and to help him deal with it once the shock of how it really was hit him."

"Oh, I don't know. I've been told otherwise." Ginny couldn't help but think about that damning letter from Lenny. He had always been so common sensible. How could he be wrong about her? Lenny's letter was never far out of Ginny's mind.

They sat and enjoyed their coffee and breakfasts in comfortable silence for a couple of minutes. Tony passed by again, and Ginny called out to him, "You were right, Tony. As good as the croissants are, the French toast is better." Tony smiled at her, but she felt it was a rather wan smile. He looked tired today. He often looked tired. But this morning he looked particularly tired.

She then turned back to Tom. The mention of the French toast had reminded her of something she wanted to ask. But she wanted to work up to it. "Did you know Anne Richards, Tom?"

"No, she was before my time here."

A moment of silence and then, "Did you know my Aunt Marie?"

Tom laughed. "Yes, of course. We all knew your Aunt Marie. She was a very nice woman."

"That's what everyone has said about her. That she was a nice woman. What does that actually mean here, for the residents of Savannah's Chatham Square?"

"I guess you could say Marie was the glue that held us together. She was Mother Confessor and Miss Sunshine all rolled into one. There was nothing any one of us couldn't take to her and then feel better about when we parted from her. We pretty much fell apart as a little community here on the square when she died. Haven't fully recovered yet, I'm afraid. But I guess we're getting there."

"Did she ever mention that she had a niece? Did she ever say anything about me? We weren't really ever that close. I think my mother—her sister—thought Marie was just a bit too risqué. She didn't want too much of that rubbing off on me. But there are times when I think not enough of that has rubbed off on me."

"Yes, she mentioned you a few times—there in the last couple of months."

"Anything you can tell me?"

"I think she was worried a bit about you. I knew that she originally was considering leaving her apartment to SCAD. To be used as visitor's accommodations. But then she said she had a niece to leave it to. Someone she said she thought needed to be here."

"She thought I needed to be here." It came out as a mere whisper and more a statement than a question. Then louder. "Even at the end she was thinking of what I needed. I'm sorry I didn't have an opportunity to know her better."

"You can take what she said two ways, you know, Ginny."

"Oh?"

"I'm not sure but what she was saying that we needed you here. And from what you did for Arnie yesterday, I'm not so sure that isn't the right interpretation."

Ginny reddened right up. This certainly wasn't what Lenny had told her in his letter.

And speaking of letters, Tom was reaching into the pocket of his jacket for his wallet and a letter fell out as well. He looked pained and then concerned and then swept it back up and stuffed it back into his pocket.

"You look like you are in pain, Tom. Is anything the matter?"

"No, not really. Well, yes, but nothing I can't handle—eventually. I got this letter and I don't know how to respond. It's not a bad something, just a conundrum. But I'll figure it out. So where were we in the conversation?"

"Nowhere really. But if we're switching gears, I have something else on my mind I'd like to talk about. Have you met the little girl living next door to me—in the basement—Samantha Johnson?"

"Certainly have. Smart little thing. Too bad about the leg."

"I worry about her. She thinks her father is down in New Orleans earning the money for an operation for her."

"Stranger things have happened. But you aren't the only one worried about her. Rose said essentially the same thing to me the other day."

"Rose? You talk with Rose."

"Yeah, sure. Don't discount Rose. Why, I could tell you things about Rose that—" But then he stopped and, embarrassed at himself, took a big swig of coffee to try to cover it up.

"Things about Rose? Like what?"

"I'm sorry, I shouldn't have said that. Rose is very particular about her privacy, and I should be respecting that. When Rose wants to warm up to you, she'll do so. On her own terms. That's always been Rose."

"She introduced herself to me the other day. Asked me if I'd help her feed the birds."

"Well, there you go. You can't get a better offer from Rose than that. She loves those birds like they were family. That's more progress than most have made."

"You mean like that grumpy man in the big house on the west side of the square."

"My lips are sealed. Say, Tony," he called out as the waiter passed their table again. "My tab, please, my fine man. My coffee break is well over at the bookstore. There will be people standing in line for their copies of *Midnight*."

Ginny thought that was a bit of a rushed retreat. She hoped she hadn't put Tom off by being too nosy. But he probably had raised more questions in her mind than the questions he'd cleared up. She just seemed to be trading one set of mysteries for another. But she was solving one or two—and not just for herself. She somehow felt very, very good about that.

"Oh good, he's gone," Tony bent down and whispered at her after Tom had paid his bill and left. "I thought he'd never leave. Run away with me, my love. And bring our Marie Antoinette doll with you. I think you are very naughty not to have brought her back to me today."

"Oh, Tony. You're being unusually chipper today."

"Chipper? I wished I felt that way."

"Yes, you do look a little down. Getting enough sleep?"

"There's never enough sleep when you're working two jobs."

"Two jobs? Where else are you working?"

"You really don't want to know."

"Try me."

"If I did, you'd probably never show up here for breakfast again."

"As I said, try me. You've looked down in the dumps off and on since I first started coming here. I know that's not the bubbly you—now that I've seen the other side of you."

"Oh, love, you haven't seen the other side of me—not by a long shot."

"As I said, try me."

48

"You're sounding like your Aunt Marie now."

"I certainly hope so. So come on. Tell me."

"Well, OK. You asked for it. Ever hear of Club One?"

"No, what's Club One?"

"See, I knew I couldn't tell you. You simply have no idea."

"Hey, I just got to Savannah. I've got a lot to learn, I know. So, tell me what Club One is."

Tony laughed now.

"What's so funny?"

"Remembering back to that day you brought Marie Antoinette in, and I told you I was Tony, short for Antoinette. You didn't get it, did you?"

"Yes, I think I did. And I'm telling you I don't care. This is Savannah and I like its 'who cares?' approach to life."

"Well, OK, love. The joke is that I really am Marie Antoinette."

"You're really Marie Antoinette."

"Yes, on stage. Club One is an impersonation club downtown. Most of the clientele are men, but there are some woman and couples who like to slum there for the thrill too. I'm one of the main acts there three nights a week. I play Marie Antoinette."

Ginny laughed for a full half minute—which told Tony that everything was all right.

"I've got to see that," she said. "You've got to get me in to see your act. I'll bet you're a slamming Marie Antoinette."

"All except for the losing her head part, darling. I don't lose my head over anything. Well, not for something as small as a revolution." And then Tony made a more serious face. "You are all right about that? Really?"

"Sure. It's your life, and I'll bet it's great entertainment."

"I wish everyone took that attitude."

"So that's it, is it? There's someone you care about who isn't OK with it?"

"About the only one I care about. My mother. My big mistake was that I moved into the club, made it my mailing address. And as soon as I did that, my momma caught on to what I was doing, I guess. Because she hasn't mailed me anything since then. I keep sending her letters, pretending nothing's wrong. And she just doesn't answer back."

"Oh, I'm sorry, Tony. That's too bad. There's always hope though, I'm sure, that she'll come around. There's nothing like mother love." There didn't seem to be anything else for Ginny to tell Tony. This was too much of a family affair for her to get into.

"But you'll let me see your act, won't you? When do you perform next?"

"Night after tomorrow. I'll get you a ticket."

Ginny went and loved it and went back at least once a week for the next three weeks. She quickly became a fixture, thanks to Tony introducing her around. She quite liked their Ethel Merman impersonator, who was a big, towering teddy bear named Harold and who more or less held down the secretarial duties at the club too. But she didn't much care for

50

the manager of the troupe playing the club. His name was Big George, and it was whispered about that he was a mean drunk and bullied his players and that he had his hand in the till.

In the third week after Ginny had started appearing at the club regularly, the "hand in the till" part apparently panned out, because Big George had absconded and the week's earnings for the troupe was missing.

During that evening while Tony was backstage getting ready for his act, Harold came over to Ginny's table.

"Is it OK if I sit and get a load off, honey?" Harold asked.

"By all means, sit, Ethel. And give it a rest. Big news about Big George, I take it. I hope you all can manage with the week's earnings being short."

"Most of our take is in tips anyway, and Big George didn't get to those," Harold said. "But there is something I'd like your advice on."

"What? How can I help?"

"You could help tell me what to do with these," Harold said. And he plopped a stack of envelopes bound in a rubber band down on the top of the table.

"Who are those to?" Ginny asked.

"Tony. They're all to Tony. Big George has been intercepting Tony's mail. He was afraid Tony's relatives were trying to get him to come home, and Tony was the big draw for the troupe. Big George didn't want to lose him. And I'm sorry to say I've known all along that Big George was holding these back. But I was told I'd be beaten and fired if I said anything. And I need this job. It's the best gig I've ever had. I feel bad about it, though. You're Tony's friend. What do you think I should do?"

"Give them to Tony," Ginny answered straight away. "Tonight. I understand your predicament. And I think Tony would too. But there's no need to get into that. Just give them to Tony and say you found them in Big George's office just now—that you've never seen them before."

"You think that'll be all right? I somehow feel that—"

"Trust me, Tony will be so happy to see those letters that he won't ask any questions. And I bet it will perk Tony right up. You'll be doing him the greatest of favors. You don't have to tell him how long you've known about them. That won't change anything. He'll just be delighted to have them."

Harold thanked Ginny and picked the letters up and headed for the backstage area.

Ginny hoped that he'd at least wait until Marie Antoinette had done her set or they'd never see the French queen on stage tonight—and apparently that was the case, because Tony appeared and was brilliant.

And the next day, when she appeared at William's Café, Tony was full of life and sass and walking on air. So Ginny was sure that had all worked out well in the end.

Chapter Five

"There now, you've got it. I think you're ready to help with Marie's smile."

"It's her eye, isn't it? It's her eye I'm putting in. You said this was the eye."

They were sitting at the workbench in Ginny's apartment. Samantha was all attention and seriousness and care, and Ginny wanted to both laugh and cry as she looked upon Samantha's concentration to get the blue pupil of the eye "just so" on the practice template.

"Yes, it's her eyes you'll be putting in—or, rather, the very center of the eye. We call that the pupil. When someone is happy, Samantha, they smile from much more than the mouth. You can see it in their eyes—and you can feel it in places you can't see."

"In places you can't see?"

"Yes. You can feel it in the heart as well. Now, it's time you gave this Marie Antoinette doll the smile in her eyes—that's what the sparkles in the paint will do. Careful now—but don't

53

worry, if it doesn't come out just right, we can take it off and do it over."

"Do it over. We can do that?"

"Yes, with dolls we can do that." Ginny knew it was time. She released the precious doll into the hands of the little girl. Then she sighed. "Sometimes I wish it was that easy to do over in real life—for people to do that."

"My mamma says people can have do overs," Samantha said without even considering what she was saying. All of her concentration was on the doll as she approached its face with the tip of the charged paint brush. "She says that's why we go to church—so we can be given do overs."

"Your mother's a wise—and patient—woman, Samantha. You're lucky to have her. There, that was perfect. Just perfect. Now, let's charge the brush with more of the glittery paint and we can do the second pupil."

"My mother smiles a lot. Even when I don't think there's anything to smile about."

"That's a gift your mother has then, Samantha. Here, here's the brush again. Turn her head just a bit that way. It's a secret of the art, but if the paint is just a bit heavier on this side, the eye will look more realistic—it will seem she's looking right back at you."

"My mamma gots a letter yesterday. It was from my daddy. She cried. But then when she saw I was there, she looked right back at me and she smiled."

Ginny had to look away. It wasn't that she couldn't bear to watch Samantha put in that last pupil—because Samantha

54

was doing it just right; her hand was steady and her aim was true. It was because she just couldn't bear to think what was in that letter from Samantha's father and what strength Samantha's mother must have needed to smile.

"I like my mamma's smile. I think she smiles from the heart. You have a nice smile too. Are you smiling in your heart?"

"I wish. I only wish." It was not what Ginny said but what she whispered inside her mind; it was what she could do no more than wish for.

* * * *

"She did a good job. See how it sparkles in the sunlight?"

"I sure do like Miss Marie Antoinette smiling more than sad," Tony said, as he looked down at the Marie Antoinette doll Ginny had taken out and propped up on its box in the café seat. Tom looked over at the doll from his adjacent seat in William's Café and smiled. "And you say that little girl, Samantha, painted on those eyes herself?"

"Yes, well the pupils, she did. And I let her do a few stitches on the hem here in back. She was delighted to do it—and just as careful as she could be. She's really a delightful little girl. I wish there was something we . . . I could do for her."

"Me too," Tom chimed in. "You can keep that 'we.' I've given her some books from the shop in exchange for some light dusting and shelving, but she deserves better than what the world is throwing at her."

"Do you think her father will ever come back?" Ginny asked.

"Not likely," Tony said with a snort. "How many men go to New Orleans to make their fortunes when they've facing off with all those folks leaving New Orleans because of the afterfall of that Hurricane Katrina. But, bite my tongue for being a spiteful bitch."

"How so?" Ginny asked, looking up at Tony, startled.

"Well, I knew of that Rodney Johnson before he left. He did blow a mean horn—down in some of the clubs downtown. And at the time of his leaving, I didn't mark him for a man who would leave his family. But then maybe he was trying and the world just got too heavy a burden for him. This ain't no make-believe world we live in. We have to do with what we got and smile at it—and accept it."

"My, that's a long, noble speech," Ginny said. "Did you hear that down at Club One?" She was glad that she had slid into a comfortable relationship with Tony like this. He was refreshing to talk to. Not that Tom wasn't nice to talk to also. She really did like meeting Tom here for breakfast—or for lunch, as she was doing today. But discussions with him were more serious—about books and art and such. And they still avoided the type of topic that Ginny increasingly was interested in getting to with Tom.

"Nope. My momma done told me that."

"Your mother?"

"Yep. In her last letter. Got it yesterday."

"Oh," Ginny said, feeling a warm glow deep down inside her. Tony indeed had been a whole new, much sunnier—and, of course, even more flamboyant—character since he'd gotten that stack of letters from his mother.

"Harold couldn't keep it in," Tony continued. "He told me it was you who told him to just march right in and give me those letters as I come off stage at Club One. You know, every day here, you seem to be more and more like that Aunt Marie of yours. And speaking, of which, look and see what we have here. Why, as I live and breathe, I do think it's you, Mr. Richards. Out and about."

Ginny and Tom looked up, surprised to see Arnie Richards outside of his apartment.

"Arnie!" Ginny exclaimed. "Please. Please come and join us. What brings you out?"

"Thanks. Don't mind if I do. A cup of that swill you call coffee here, Tony, if you please. What brings me out? Well, that doctor you got me to—thanks, Tom, for taking me there—said that as soon as I could put weight on my foot without my ankle wincing, I'd best give it some exercise or it will lock up on me. And this far is about all the exercise I could manage today."

"Here, here, sit by Marie Antoinette."

"It's a beautiful doll, Ginny. Did you say you were going to let that little girl, Samantha, help you finish it out?"

"I did. And if you can't tell what she did to it, then I guess she did a very good job."

"Think she'll grow up to be an artist?"

"She wants to be a doctor," Ginny said.

"Too bad. Not much of a chance of that with the beginning she's getting," Arnie said.

"More the pity that," Tom interjected. "I just wish there was something that could be done for that leg of hers."

"There is, of course," Ginny said.

"But can you imagine the money it would take for that?" Tom said.

Arnie reentered the conversation in a thoughtful mode. "I know a surgeon here—but, no, that would still take a small fortune. That's too high a dream."

"Are any dreams truly too high?" Tom asked. Ginny saw his hand move to the inner pocket of his jacket and half pull an envelope from there. She wondered if it was the same letter he'd referred to the other day—and, if so, why he was still carrying it around. This wasn't the same jacket.

And when she thought of the jacket, it occurred to her that she was shivering a bit, in spite of the sweater she was wearing. It was usually OK out here, but occasionally a breeze went through that reminded her that she'd been told not to toss all of her fall and winter things when she'd moved down here from Richmond—that it could get pretty cool in Savannah later in the year too.

But then she was struck by how this bantering conversation was running much deeper than she realized when Arnie said, "Some dreams—when they reach too high—can bring all dreaming crashing down where some smaller dreams might have been achieved if you just didn't aim too high. I gave up dreaming some time ago."

"But it's never really too late to start building dreams up again, is it?" Tom asked in a soft voice.

"For some people . . . sometimes . . . I think it is." Arnie answered.

And Ginny knew it was Anne he was thinking of, and she reached out and took Arnie's hand in hers . . . and he let her.

"So, what's in the other box?" Tony was back and the sun overhead must have broken free from a cloud, because he was standing in a beam of light and Ginny didn't feel the chill in the air anymore.

"The other box? Oh that. The box here next to Marie Antoinette in the chair. That's another doll. I'm taking them to display at the college—showing the range of subjects you can do with dolls. A reporter from the *Savannah Morning News* is supposed to come down to cover our new exhibits."

"So, the other doll isn't a tragic historical queen destined to lose her head?"

"A queen of sorts—at least from around here," Ginny said with a giggle. "Here, I'll show you. You can tell me who that is." She opened the box and set the second doll down beside the Marie Antoinette doll in the chair. "There. Who is it?"

Tony was laughing as Tom and Arnie leaned over, scrutinizing the doll of an entirely different time and place as the first one, and shook their heads.

"I don't know. You, Tom?" Arnie said.

"Haven't a clue, although it does look strangely familiar," Tom answered.

Tony was still laughing.

"Tell them who that is, Tony," she said, knowing he would know.

"Why, honey childs, that spatula she's got in her hand done gave it away. That's our very own Paula Deen."

"Oh, that's right," Tom said. "I should have seen it."

Arnie still looked perplexed.

"She's our local cooking and restaurant maven," Tom explained to Arnie. "Owns restaurants all over the place and shows up all over TV cooking programs. One of our living legends. You *haven't* been out for a while, have you, Arnie? Good job, Ginny. I didn't know you could have so much fun with these dolls."

They all heard the snort and looked up as the man from the Greek Revival pile on the west side of the square walked by with a bunch of letters in his hand. There was a mailbox down at the corner he was headed toward.

"Ah, Mr. Grump," Ginny said after he'd passed by.

"Who? Mr. Winthrop?" Arnie spoke up. "Oh, he's pretty blunt, but he's a fine man."

"More reclusive and a bit eccentric, I'd say," Tom piped in. "He comes in the bookstore frequently. We carry his books."

"His books?" Ginny was a little bewildered.

"Don't tell me you haven't heard of his poetry," Tony chimed in as he started clearing the table of debris. "He's

Clayton Winthrop. His poetry is absolutely dreamy. Don't see him much outside his house, though."

"That's the poet Clayton Winthrop?" Ginny asked in disbelief.

"Yep. Pretty scary, isn't it?" Tony chirped "I'll bet you imagined someone looking like Lord Byron. I'll have to admit that would have been nice."

"Well, I hadn't imagined someone who had been so short with me when I passed him in front of his house would write sensitive poetry."

"He's a bit prickly, but mostly harmless," Tom said. "He's been disappointed in love and isn't too trusting anymore. You can see it in his poetry when you read closely. A tragic love affair, I understand. Jilted on the way to that altar— dumped while he was off fighting in Vietnam."

"And he has a heart of gold," Arnie added. "His family owned the import business that bailed Anne and me out in Kenya. That's how we got to the States—why we settled here in Savannah. He was a good and fair employer. He treated us well."

Ginny was still processing that as Winthrop was passing back by the café after mailing his letter.

"Hello there, Mr. Winthrop," Tom called out to him. "Care to join us for a cup of coffee and some chat?"

"Yes, please do," Arnie chimed in. "I don't think you've properly met our Ginny here."

Winthrop stopped, dead in his tracks, clearly startled by the invitation. But pleased too. You could see that creep across his face. "Uh, thanks, Tom. Arnie. I believe I'd like that."

"Mr. Winthrop," Tom was saying as the elderly man approached the table and Ginny was boxing up her dolls and moving them to a chair at an adjacent free table, "This is Ginny, a fairly new resident here. She's Marie Purcell's niece. You remember Marie. Ginny's living in Marie's apartment."

"Marie. Oh my, oh yes, I remember Marie. A great woman—and friend—was Marie."

As Clayton Winthrop settled in—as they all settled back in as if they were life-long friends—Ginny's thoughts went to Rose and why Clayton Winthrop had been so adamantly down on her. And when Ginny's thoughts went to Rose, she realized that the breeze had come up again and she was clutching her sweater about her. It would get colder than this—much colder—before it started turning warm again in Savannah. Ginny was worried about Rose and what she would do in the colder months—even where she spent her nights even now. So many worries. So little Ginny could do about it. She wondered what Marie would do.

Chapter Six

"It would just be for the cold months. I have plenty of room."

"Thanks for asking, Ginny. But no, no thank you. I can manage. I've always had more than enough."

Rose and Ginny were out in the Chatham Square park—sitting on the same bench. Rose was busy mixing and matching her bits of cloth around her two-thirds of the bench—she'd invited Ginny to sit with her, but she had remained in command of the bench—as Ginny had just finished feeding bread crumbs to the birds and was beginning to take up the sewing of the skirt for a new doll, one she'd been commissioned to do.

"But it's going to get colder—or so I've been told."

"I dress plenty warm."

"I know you do. But I worry about you out in the cold at night. And I have a perfectly fine single bed in my workroom—a studio couch, but it has a good mattress. I'd be the happier. I'd be the happier knowing you were inside, safe at night. At least for the colder months."

"Thanks. But I have my routine. I've had it for years and it works quite well for me. I live in a mansion."

Ginny was perplexed and then she looked at Rose, whose gaze was looking up and around and scanning from west to east in Chatham Square. And then Ginny had to laugh, as this, indeed, was a mansion they all lived in here in this square. The Fan district of Richmond had been very nice, but Ginny hadn't seen anything to compare with Savannah's generous pattern of squares and parks for livability.

They sat, quietly, companionable, as Ginny began to sew and Rose continued mixing and matching swatches and humming to herself in a deep, rich contralto voice.

It was Rose who broke into the mood.

"You know she offered me that room too."

"She?"

"Yes, your Aunt Marie. She said she was worried for me too. A fine woman, your Aunt Marie. And she had me going there for a short while. And when I didn't budge, do you know what she said?"

"No, what?"

"She said she wanted me to meet her niece sometime. I didn't know what that meant then, but I think I do now. Thanks for the offer, but I'll have to pass. There are people in this world who need help. But I'm not one of them."

As she said this, Ginny felt Rose was speaking with some deeper meaning, and she looked up and saw that Rose was staring across the park—at Samantha Johnson, just struggling home from school under a backpack filled with books that looked like it was almost as big as she was.

"Ah, Samantha. Yes, she is a worry, isn't she?" Ginny murmured.

"These things have a way of working themselves out. Sometimes time heals. And then sometimes it doesn't." Rose gave a snort at that.

"I feel so sad for her. She told me that her mother received a letter from her father and cried. Someone was talking at lunch today about some dreams being just too big— that maybe we should settle for smaller dreams. Do you think Samantha's dream of her father sweeping back in and solving all of her problems is a dream that's too big?"

"Well, having a father by your side, rich or not, is quite a comfort. But problems? There are no end to those. Happily, there's no end to solutions too. As for Samantha's father, I'm sure she would be a happy girl just to have him home again."

"Do you think that will ever happen?"

"You mentioned her mother getting a letter from her father and crying. You know letters can go two ways and anyone can send a letter. I could see that there might be some crying going on at her father's end of the letter chain too. And not all crying is bad. Some of it can be a joy."

Ginny looked over at Rose, who was smiling a little smile and started humming again and rocking back and forth, her hands shuffling pieces of cloth back and forth and comparing and holding them up against each other.

It was just Rose's way, Ginny was beginning to understand. She was a strongly independent, stubborn, and eccentric woman. There was no telling what she'd say or do. She'd be making complete sense at one moment and then fly off into something completely incomprehensible. And obviously that was the way she wanted to live her life; Ginny would just have to let her be.

Rose suddenly stopped humming and almost blurted out her next statement. "I think our Samantha there will be a stronger young woman for the childhood she's having. I think in the long run it will be good for her."

"I suppose," Ginny answered. The tone of her voice was full of doubt.

"And you. I sense that you have some sadness in your life, Ginny. Don't you think it has made you stronger?"

Ginny didn't say anything, but she had to admit to herself that it was something to think about. But as the silence stretched out, it was something entirely different that entered her mind—and then begged to be let out.

"Rose. Clapton Winthrop from the house over there. He seems to hold a grudge against you, and I can't—"

"Ah you've met our resident poet, have you? And I don't mean that in a derogatory sense. He's a fine poet."

"Yes, but—"

"And he told you to stay away from the Wicked Witch of the Park, I suppose."

"Well, yes, if not exactly in those words. He was pretty vehement about it."

"He's entitled, I guess."

"I don't understand."

Rose sighed and put down the swatches of cloth she had been holding up to the sunlight filtering through the sheltering limbs of the tall trees and dug into a worn leather valise wedged between her and Ginny. "Well, if we are on shared bird-feeding relations, I guess you should be privy to the deepest, darkest secret of Chatham Square," she said, as she drew forth a yellow, folded over sheet of paper.

She didn't open it or hand it over immediately, though.

"Have you heard of Clayton Winthrop's tragedy?"

"Perhaps. I've been told of one, yes."

"How he was jilted—spurned by his intended while he was overseas fighting for his country?"

"Yes. Yes, that's essentially what I heard."

"Well, would it surprise you to know I was the intended who was said to have spurned him?"

"You?" The surprise was just too complete and sudden. Ginny couldn't hold back the gasp.

"Yes me, funny, isn't it? A gasp is the best response. I quite agree. This old wreck was once a beauty who launched a thousand love poems." Rose's accompanying laugh was deep, melodic—but it also had an edge of irony and bitterness to it.

"Oh, Rose. I didn't know. I don't know what—"

"It was bad, sticky, yes. But I'm not quite that monster. At least I was trying not to be. Here, read this, please."

Ginny took the folded paper from Rose's hand and opened it and read, the revelation of what it revealed nearly taking her breath away.

"Why. Why, Rose. This is a death notice."

"Yep. An official one from the president of the United States himself. Can you see the name of the deceased?"

"Yes. It says 'Clayton Winthrop.'"

It took a moment for the significance of the letter to sink in, and Rose just sat there, fiddling with her swatches of cloth and eying Ginny's reaction as she watch it all get processed in Ginny's mind.

"So . . . so . . . they notified you he was dead . . . in combat."

"Not me. His mother. But she gave it to me. It killed her. So, when Clay came back from war, he came back not only to a mother's grave—his father had died long before that—but to a woman who was married to another man. And not just to another man, but to Clay's best friend."

"He didn't . . . he didn't know about the letter? That he had been declared dead?"

"No. Not then, and not now."

"But, why didn't you—?"

"By then I'd married Clay's best friend. We'd all come up together. Attended the same arts school. Clay with his poetry, and Stephen his painting. It had been the three of us, twisted together, for years. Important, formative years. Stephen didn't declare his love until after we thought Clay was gone. And I liked Stephen a lot, and we had even more in common

68

after this letter—a shared grief. And I can't say I didn't fall in love with Stephen—just watching the effect of Clay's supposed death on Stephen and how he comforted me was enough for me to fall in love with Stephen. I didn't fall out of love with Clay. But he was dead. And then when he wasn't dead, there wasn't really anything we could do to go back—to erase what we'd all become. It wasn't Clay's fault, and it certainly wasn't Stephen's fault. The best I could do was to make it my fault. So I did. And that is that. After Stephen died, both Clay and I were too old to bring it up again. And I was . . . well you can see for yourself what I have become."

"And you've never—?"

"No. Some things are best left to lie."

"I suppose," Ginny said. But, in fact, she supposed nothing of the sort. Rose had taken the letter back and buried it in the valise under bits of cloth. But when she wasn't looking, Ginny fished it out and hid it in her sewing basket. She had experienced the havoc that one letter from a war zone had done in her life. She saw no reason why one should do the same in Rose's life forever.

She'd met Clayton Winthrop now. He was a very nice man—just with an edge of bitterness. Ginny may not be able to put these two together again, but even though Rose had apparently come to an accommodation to this kick in the stomach from life, there was no reason Clayton Winthrop needed to live in perpetual falsely based bitterness. Ginny decided she would Xerox the death notice and slip the original back in Rose's valise by tomorrow. And someday. Ginny didn't know how or when or under what circumstances. But someday, Clayton Winthrop would get an answer to questions that had been eating away at him far too long.

Rose's propensity to flit from topic to topic pulled Ginny out of her scheming thoughts. "I'm hungry. You wouldn't happen to have another half of a sandwich in there, would you?"

Ginny jerked, startled in guilt by Rose pawing at the sewing basket where she'd just hidden the death notice.

"No, I don't. But, if you'd like we could go over there to William's Café."

"Your treat?" Rose asked. And then when Ginny looked at her sharply, Rose let loose a delighted "gotcha" cackle.

"Sure," Ginny answered. "But maybe someone else will come along who we can stick the bill with."

Rose cackled again.

Chapter Seven

Ginny was amazed. She'd only lived in Chatham Square for two months now. And she'd started off so lonely and wondered where all the friendly people of Savannah were. And here she was now, sitting in the open air of William's Café—amid an abundance of fast friends. And a pleasantly motley crew it was. She couldn't have asked for a more interesting collection of characters. All residents of—or at least working full time in—the square; a small, tight community within a fascinating southern city.

Even Rose was here. Not only Rose, but Clayton Winthrop was here as well. They were sitting as far away from each other as possible at the two wrought-iron tables the others had dragged together—and they didn't speak directly to each other. But they weren't throwing up tension into the air either. They were being as comfortable as the rest of the little community that had come together.

Tom and Arnie were there, of course, and even Tony had pulled up a chair. They were practically the only ones in the café at this time of afternoon—in the waning sunlight, just before twilight set in. Ginny's favorite time of the day. And it had been unseasonably warm today. Today a sweater was enough, and Ginny found she didn't even have to snuggle deep into it to stay comfortable. Just the proximity of her new friends provided all the warmth she needed. There was, miraculously, another waiter on duty—the first time Ginny had seen anyone working here other than Tony. And Tony had said he'd take care of this table if the other waiter took care of any other business that showed up.

They weren't all there. The whole community wasn't there. Samantha Johnson wasn't there. But Samantha was nearby—out in the park, sitting primly on Rose's bench and making a doll—not from anything Ginny had given her. But she was making a doll from what she'd found herself. Ginny had seen it up close earlier in the day, though, and she could have sworn she'd seen some of that material in what Rose had been shuffling about the previous day.

Even though Samantha wasn't there, in person, among them, Samantha was very much in the center of this community that had gathered—not by appointment, but by slowly coalescing circumstance—around Ginny and Rose. The two had been coming out of the park here now for several days after feeding the birds, with Ginny making sure that Rose had something to eat before she went in to her own dinner—and on this afternoon, all of the others just naturally drifted in and sat down. One of the nice things about the café's outside tables was that the area could be seen from anywhere else in the square.

72

"Really something should be done. As I was telling Ginny and Tom the other day, I know a surgeon who I'm sure would donate his services—he's done that before. That wouldn't come close to covering it—but it's a start. And you have to start somewhere." It was Arnie who said that, and Ginny was pleased at his mention of starting from somewhere. Tom had told Arnie the same thing about dreams the other day. Arnie had brushed that aside then, but obviously he had been doing some thinking about it—even if he didn't consciously realize he had.

"That was nice of you to say what you did about Samantha in the interview the newspaper did on your doll exhibit yesterday, Ginny." That was Clayton Winthrop. His voice was warm with praise, and Ginny didn't know why she'd ever thought of him as a grumpy old man.

"Yes, you made it sound like she'd practically made the Marie Antoinette doll all by herself," Tom chimed in.

"Well, she did help," Ginny said. "I always thought that getting the pupil of the eyes just right was what brought the dolls to life—and she's the one who could see that the original face would be a disaster. But, I agree. I do wish there was something we . . . I could do about that."

"Let's stick with the 'we,'" Arnie put in, and Ginny harkened back to the same statement she'd heard days ago. It struck her that she'd been talking about this but not really doing anything, and she was resolved that today, here, was where something would start being done about this. Arnie was still talking, though, so she didn't declare her intent. In fact, she didn't have a chance to. "A 'we' can do far more than an 'I,' if they stick together."

"I've been thinking about that," Tony said, a serious tone to his voice that arrested the attention of all. "I think Club One would be willing to do a special performance with all the proceeds going to an operation for Samantha. Again, it wouldn't do all that was needed, but this is Savannah. It loves its impersonation revues. I'm sure the publicity alone would bring in money if we established a fund."

The group broke into murmurs of side conversation until Tom's voice rang out over the hubbub. "I've been thinking too." As he said this, he pulled that letter out of the inside pocket of his jacket that Ginny had seen him nervously fingering for months.

Everyone looked at him in expectation and curiosity. He was looking even more serious than Tony had.

"I've had this letter for a while, and I've had no idea what to do about it. It's from a publisher. I helped a man write a book—well, I pretty much ghosted it. I provide books to the prison and go along and have a discussion group with some of the prisoners. There was an interesting man there, a man who started into the prison system many years ago from being arrested and beaten for civil rights activity. From there, though, he went deeper into a life of crime. And then, in prison, he turned all that around and started helping other inmates change their perspectives on the world too. Well, I found what he had to say about that inspirational. And I encouraged him to write a book about it. And he did—or, rather, it turned out that we did.

And then he died, without leaving anyone behind—or anything behind but this manuscript, which he willed to me. So I sent it to a publisher. And he's publishing it and tells me it should do well in the marketplace."

"That sounds wonderful, Tom," Ginny said. "But I don't know what the problem is—how that fits—"

"I don't feel right profiting from that. I helped him get it written because of the message he had to give, not because I was looking to profit from it financially. I've thought that whatever came out of it should go to helping someone out, helping them rise above what that man wasn't able to, wasn't given the opportunity to. And now we have this possibility with Samantha. It seems like more a blessing than any sort of loss for me. I'd like to put whatever comes out of that book to Samantha's needs."

Silence reigned for several minutes before Rose broke the spell. "That's a marvelous thing for you to do, Tom. And I like Tony's special performance idea too. As he said, it's not just what can be made off the event. The publicity off it can add even more. I think I can get the Armstrong Inn here on the square to do a special dinner and donate the proceeds as well."

Ginny looked at Rose in surprise. "You think you can get the Armstrong Inn to do that?"

Tony laughed. "Girl, I don't think you know the half of what our Rose here can do."

Before Ginny could speak up again, Arnie was speaking. "It's not much, and not directly of help. But . . . as well as trying to get my surgeon friend on board, I could let

Samantha and her mother move over to the basement apartment under me, rent free. That would free up some of their cash flow."

"Arnie!" Ginny said sharply.

"Sorry, Ginny. You moved in during my niggardly phase. Sorry I didn't tell you I owned the apartment—that I picked it up on the foreclosure sale. I'll pay another share for those repairs too."

Ginny laughed and Arnie ducked back into the background again, grateful to escape without a reprimand.

Everyone settled down again. Tony had gone back into the restaurant and reappeared with a gaggle of wine bottles. The other waiter swam along in his wake juggling a tray of wine glasses. "And by my own leave," Tony sang out gaily, "I declare that William's Café will contribute its mite in the form of refreshments for the planning committee."

"I guess that leaves me," Ginny said. "Strangely enough I've been giving it thought too—I just needed a fire lit under me to get it going. The publicity for my doll exhibition has been good—and it was nice of them to mention Samantha. It seems natural, taking advantage of this, that I sell off Marie Antoinette and another doll or two—maybe at auction—and contribute that to the cause."

"But that could be thousands of dollars," Tom said with a gasp.

"If your book does well, that will be thousands of dollars too—as would most of the other ideas that have been offered up, all of which we can do as a team. But I think of Marie

Antoinette as Samantha's doll now anyway, and I have loads of materials. Most of the expense is in what I put into them with my time and effort. And I love the work. It would even be good publicity for orders for dolls. I've been thinking. If Tom let us put them in the window of the bookstore and we got some publicity and someone to handle a silent auction, I think it would work."

"Sounds lovely to me," said Tony. "I only wish I could bid on Marie Antoinette. May I suggest that if you auction another doll too, that it be Paula Deen. You could get top dollar for her in Savannah—probably more than anywhere else in the country—and maybe some good publicity from the non-porcelain Paula."

"Good idea," Ginny said.

"No problem with putting them in the shop window," Tom chimed in. "They'll help bring in business."

"That leaves me too, though," Clayton said. He'd been sitting in the shadows. "I have some ideas I'll work on myself, but I'd be happy to see that it all gets publicized well—and I'll write a couple of little ditties to go along with the dolls. And I can arrange for an auctioneer."

Business satisfactorily concluded, the group sank into the wine and the crackers and cheese that were just now appearing. Slowly, as dark settled in, the members of the motley Chatham Square community started drifting off—until there was only Ginny and Rose sitting at their table once more.

"What a nice group of people," Ginny said.

"Yes. They all come together well," Rose answered. "I think we are becoming again what we once were before your

Aunt Marie passed on. This is just the sort of thing that would happen when she was here. And she'd just float through it all. You wouldn't even have known what she'd done until it all blossomed forth into something wonderful."

"I wish I had known her better."

"I get the impression she knew you pretty well."

"I don't . . . I don't know what that means, Rose."

"Someday I think you will. But it's not something you can be told. It's something you have to realize for yourself. Give it time, dear. We have plenty of that here. This is Savannah; we move to our own clock—and calendar here."

"Rose."

"Yes, dear?"

"I wish you'd come home with me tonight and sleep in my workroom. It has a very nice studio bed."

"What sort of cover does it have on it?"

"Cover? Oh, I don't know. I think it's some sort of madras Indian cotton I picked up somewhere."

"Maybe when it has a nice quilt or something on it, Ginny. No, sorry, I'm teasing you. And that's not nice. Thank you again, but I can manage."

Ginny sighed. "OK, I guess we can't solve all of life's little problems in a day. I guess I should be satisfied that we have made a start with Samantha."

"You'll never solve all of life's problems, Ginny, or even see that all of its little mysteries are neatly worked out. For all its fairytale presence, Chatham Square is no different from the rest of the world. Life's mysteries just keep rolling on, and as old problems get solved, new ones arise. And wouldn't it be a dull world if it were otherwise?"

"Yes, I guess," Ginny answered, hoping her tone wasn't too petulant.

"You suffer from being too young, my dear. When you are my age, you will see it clearly. But then maybe not. Your Aunt Marie never let it slow her down. She was a dreamer of big dreams to the end."

* * * *

All of the events dedicated to Samantha's surgery were a huge success, and the surgeon Arnie enlisted busied himself with plans for what lay ahead. Savannah had responded to the call as cultured, caring southern cities were known to do. Ginny's dolls alone had brought in a bundle, Marie Antoinette having gone for nearly $10,000 and the Paula Deen doll taken away for a whopping $15,000. Neither of the buyers had been identified.

The leaves were falling from the trees in Chatham Square on a cool afternoon, as they do even in Savannah, as Rose and Ginny sat out on their bench, each contentedly working on their own specialties.

Ginny had managed to copy the death notice for the still-living Clayton Winthrop and had slipped it back in Rose's valise. Rose had said nothing about it in the interim, so Ginny felt she was safe on that score. She had no idea when or how she would make sure that Clayton saw the Xerox of that letter and at least start to see the issue from Rose's perspective. But

Ginny knew she would do that someday, even if Rose couldn't forgive her for doing it.

As Rose hummed and rocked away and played with her swatches, Ginny watched a car slowly drive around the street bordering the square and stop in front of Clayton's house. Ginny recognized the car and then the driver who emerged from it. It was the auctioneer who had handled the sales of her two dolls. As he moved up the walk to Clayton's front door, Ginny recognized the box he was carrying under his arm. It was the box she had put Marie Antoinette in when she had given the dolls to the auctioneer for delivery to their secret buyers. Ginny now knew what other "little ideas" Clayton Winthrop had had in mind concerning what he could do to contribute to the cause.

She shivered—but only partly from the delicious revelation that made her heart swell. She realized also that it was getting distinctively chilly out here.

"I think I'd best go in, Rose. And you too."

"I'll be in shortly, child," Rose said. "I have a bit more work to do here."

Arnie was waiting for her—not too patiently either—when Ginny climbed the front steps to the co-op and entered their shared foyer.

"This came for you," he said, hardly able to stifle a big grin. He was holding out a bulking bundle not too expertly covered in brown paper. "And this letter came with it."

Ginny opened the envelope and pulled out a noticeably expensive-feeling sheet of letter paper, written in an elegant hand:

I hope this will suit for a "perfectly fine" studio bed.

I feel I deserve only the finest, you know.

I call this design Chatham Square. Because it's just like our community. Each part is an individual, with a mixture of the good and the bad, but always an interesting mixture adding up to someone valuable, someone worth knowing and cherishing. And all fitting together in a whole that is even more valuable and interesting than the sum of its parts.

Dazzled, but perplexed, tears already forming in her eyes, Ginny took up the bundle and tore at the wrapping. And then she sank into the straight chair by the side table in the foyer and laughed and laughed—and cried.

Inside the package was a patchwork quilt. A lovely, intricately and expertly sewn patchwork quilt, with all of the intricate swaths of material seemingly disproportionate and wildly unique—but somehow all fitting into a perfect, lovely whole. And each of the pieces of material were something she recognized from Rose's mad collection of bits and pieces.

Chapter Eight

"It's going to get seriously cold out here in a week or two," Ginny said.

"It doesn't get seriously anything in Savannah, Ginny. You just haven't been here long enough. It will be cold for a while and then we'll have one of the most glorious spring-like days you'd ever want to see—right in the middle of December. Then when it gets only slightly cool again, we think we're in Alaska," Rose replied.

"Well, I hope we have one of those glorious days tomorrow, because Tom says he'll take me out to Tybee Island. I'd like to at least dip my toes in the ocean. I've been here for nearly three months now, and I haven't been out of the city, much less to the ocean. I've got to get a car."

"What do you need with an automobile now, young lady? It's just a drain. And where would you put it? When you need to go someplace, you can get a young man to take you there. You're quite attractive—when you smile."

"Thanks, Rose. But I like being independent. I don't want to rely on anyone else."

"We all need to rely on someone else, Ginny. It's the first lesson in being able to be reliable to someone else. You have to know the value of it."

"And who do you rely on, Rose?"

"Me? Well, I'm the exception, of course."

"So, do you think Tom Thornton is reliable?"

"Are you asking for permission to do something, young lady?"

"No, no, of course not."

"Well, I think Tom is probably more reliable than the next man. He's a fine young man. But—and I hesitate to say this—I wouldn't be putting too much stock in Tom Thornton, if I were you. At least in the way I think you might mean."

"You wouldn't?" Ginny said, surprised. She turned toward Rose to speak, but Rose was already off on some other tangent. She was looking toward the townhouse row on the south end of the square.

Ginny looked over there, but she didn't see anything. Rose apparently didn't either, because she sighed and started to hum and rock again and picked up a couple of uneven squares of mismatched material from the piles stacked around her on the bench.

Now what Rose was doing didn't look so crazy and meaningless to Ginny. Now she knew Rose was working on piecing together another quilt. The one she'd made for Ginny was brilliant in execution. Ginny could have displayed it with pride at the college of art and design. In fact, she hoped to show that one and more of Rose's work—just as soon as she could convince Rose they were art. Ginny had no idea how Rose got them sown so professionally and finished off. This woman continued to be not just a mystery but a revelation to Ginny.

And that was not destined to stop in the ensuing minutes.

"Is the room OK, Rose? Is there anything more I can provide for your comfort?"

"You've asked me that a thousand times, Ginny. Yes, it's fine. It's not the palatial suite I'm accustomed to, of course, but I couldn't snub your hospitality, now could I? This is Savannah. Ladies know how to treat other ladies here."

"You refused the offer when Aunt Marie extended it to you," Ginny said, comfortable enough with Rose to be playful. "At least that's what you told me."

"Well, she didn't have a nice patchwork quilt on the bed—and, besides, she was from Savannah. We use our manners for the northern ladies more than for each other. It appears to be more polite, but we know we're just putting the northern ladies in their place."

"Richmond is hardly in the north, Rose."

"*Charleston* is north of Savannah," Rose countered. "And any farther south than Savannah is just people from Canada and New Jersey who wished they lived in the south."

They worked, each on their separate projects for a couple of minutes in comfortable silence—except for Rose's rich contralto humming. Ginny was working on a Savannah doll now. She'd been commissioned to design one. Once she'd done so, students at the college would make as many as the shops of Savannah could absorb, and that way Ginny would be helping them cover their expenses at college.

"That's a pretty tune, Rose. What's the name of it?"

"I don't rightly remember. I've written so many tunes, you know. And sung them all over Savannah—and even down in New Orleans."

"And on the moon too, I suppose," Ginny chimed in. She was happy to go along with this sort of banter. This was normal Rose fare when she was clicking along on all cylinders.

"I've been over the moon once or twice, yes. I might have stopped there when my folks sent me on my grand tour of Europe."

"I'd settle for that trip to Tybee Island," Ginny said.

"Well, you go there with Tom regardless of the weather. Just don't get your hopes up too much in that department."

Ginny caught Rose looking hard over at the south-side town houses again.

"What are you looking at, Rose?"

"Oh, nothing much."

"Samantha should be home soon from school. Is that who you are looking for?"

"Samantha's been home a good twenty minutes or so. I saw her arrive."

"You were talking to Arnie about the operation this morning down in the foyer. Do you know if they have a date yet?"

"Next week. She goes in on Monday. They operate on Wednesday. She'll be up and about by Friday, I think, but they'll come looking for their money on Thursday."

"Oh, Rose. You're so cynical."

"Or maybe they'll come for the money on Tuesday before they'll operate on Wednesday." Rose cackled at that adjustment in the schedule.

"Oh, Rose."

Silence for a few minutes.

"Well, I hope there's enough."

"One way or the other, I'm sure there will be enough," Rose said.

"I certainly hope you're right. Oh, there you go, looking over there again. What do you . . . Oh, it's a taxi. Stopping right there. What is it, Rose? You're smiling. Who's the man who's gotten out of the taxi. Do you know him?"

"Yes, I know him, Ginny. And so do you, though you've never met him in person. Look harder. Dream bigger."

Ginny did look harder. And of course she knew who he was. He was standing tall and straight and proud, dressed just as spiffily as he could be. And in one hand was a suitcase and in the other hand . . . a trumpet case.

"Why it's Samantha's father, Rodney Johnson, isn't it? And he's smiling. Maybe he's come home as promised—with money to burn." Ginny was trying to be funny, but only to hide how choked up she'd become—although the crack in her voice gave her away on that score.

"Yes, I suppose he's come home with something to add to the coffers," Rose said in a low voice that revealed its share of emotion. "But that hardly matters, does it? He's home. And from the way Samantha and her mother are racing up those basement stairs, I think he's welcome."

They watched for several minutes—after the taxi had left and for a few minutes beyond when the Johnson family had disappeared down into the basement apartment.

"You knew, didn't you, Rose? You knew."

"Rose knows a lot, Ginny. I'll have to admit that not much of anything escapes my notice in Chatham Square. It's the burden of being the queen of the square. Like I noticed you slipping that letter of mine out of my satchel and then back in again. I don't suppose you knew I'd seen you do that."

"Oh, Rose, I'm so sorry. I don't mean to meddle, but—"

"It's OK if you show that to Clayton and tell him, Ginny. I would have done that years ago myself, but I just couldn't face up to the scene—not the scene that would get me close enough to him to show it to him and try to explain. And not for any scene that happened after that. All of that is too far gone in the past now. But I thought about it, and you're right. Oh, I know you didn't say it, but I knew you were thinking it. You're right that probably the cruelest thing was to let him fester on not knowing the full circumstance all these years. So, go ahead and tell him when and if you think it will do any good. Just don't tell me when you've done it. And don't expect it to change anything. At least from my side. It's just been too long."

"Again I'm sorry Rose. I should have asked . . . but he really can be very nice. I think he just needs this burden lifted. You, know, I think he was the one who bought the Marie Antoinette doll at auction. And he didn't say a thing about it."

"Yes, I rather thought he had bought the doll," Rose said. "I never thought there was anything bad about Clayton. I never thought any of this was his fault. He didn't even choose to go to war. But not to change the subject, even if I were to want to change the subject, but we were talking about coming home before."

"Yes?" Ginny asked, turning her eyes on Rose.

"And you were talking about buying an automobile. Does that mean you are thinking of us here, in Chatham Square, as home now."

Ginny hesitated for a moment, not really having thought about it before. But thinking about it now only came up with one answer. "Yes, I guess I do."

"Good," Rose said. "Now, could you move a bit to your left on the bench, dear? You're soaking up my light."

* * * *

Ginny was still blushing from the feeling of being a little girl whose hand was caught in the cookie jar on the letter she had been caught purloining from Rose as she walked through the park toward the Pitt Bookstore. And she was even more perplexed about Rose's cryptic remarks about Tom.

She found Tom sitting behind the desk, looking distracted. His desk was clean except for an envelope sitting, precisely lined up on the desktop in front of him.

She had to greet him twice before he looked up.

"Oh, hello, Ginny. Yes, I'm OK. I'm fine . . . well, no I'm not, actually."

"What's wrong, Tom? Is it that letter? Is the publisher rejecting the book after all? You know, that's OK. I think we'll have enough . . . and did you know Samantha's father has come home? And I think he may have come home with some money to help."

"Samantha's father's arrived. Good. Rose told me—"

"Rose told you Samantha's father was coming? How—?"

"Oh, Rose has her ways. There's so much about Rose you should know. But Rose is the one who should tell you."

Frustrated and more than slightly irritated now, Ginny blurted out, "And did you tell Rose what's the matter with you? Why you are so unhappy now?"

"Yes. Yes, I did."

"And she told you what you should do about it?"

"Yes."

"Which was?"

"She told me I should go to him. And I know she's right. It's just such a shock."

And now there was shock enough to go around inside the bookstore.

"I think I'd better sit down," Ginny said, suddenly feeling weak in the knees. But she didn't need a genie to tell her the essence of the problem here—or why Rose had tried to warn her off just now.

The first part of what Tom had to say was the hardest and the most uncomfortable for both of them—although Tom's discomfort might have been magnified if he'd had any idea how Ginny had been taking his interest in her and her work.

"He found out up in Washington, D.C. He's on sabbatical at the Corcoran. A sabbatical from SCAD. You're occupying his slot there, actually."

It took a moment for Ginny to get rebalanced from the double whammy. Tom must have known all along that she was in her boyfriend's position at the college—and yet he'd still been as nice to her as he could be. But that was the lesser of the two revelations she had to deal with here. "They're sure? He's had a second opinion?"

"And a third and maybe even a fourth, if I know him. He went through all the testing without telling me. He didn't want to concern me until it was all confirmed."

"But it's not AIDs?"

"No, it's not that. He's not young. That wasn't his first heart attack. And he's had all of the replacement of all those parts he can have. He's just old. I shouldn't have fallen in love with a much older man."

"We don't have choices about those things. Tom."

"No, I suppose not. And I'm just being silly. We had ten good years."

"But you say he doesn't want you to come to Washington?"

"No. He says I should go on with my life. That there's nothing for me to do there, he says. He's not going to fight it.

90

He told me he's aged considerably during the testing. He doesn't want me to see him that way."

"And Rose told you you should ignore him and go?"

"Yes."

"I'm with Rose."

"Thank you, Ginny. I knew you'd understand." But after a moment's pause, he frowned, the magnitude of it all sinking further in. "But there's so much to do. There are arrangements, and the shop needs to be covered. And I'm driving you out to Tybee Island tomorrow. I know you've been looking forward to that. So have I."

"But you want to go, don't you? Now."

"Yes." It was just a whisper.

"You have two shop assistants. Give me their numbers and I'll get them in here to cover until you can decide what you need to do long term. Tybee Island isn't going anywhere. I'll see it some day. Go get in your car and start driving north."

"Thank you, Ginny. Thank you. I look at you and I hear your Aunt Marie speaking. It's not just the tone of your voice. It's her common sense and her sensitivity, cutting right through everything. Thank you."

Ginny stood at the window and watched him moving swiftly, if in a confused, rambling sort of way, toward where he had his car parked. Her heart wasn't breaking, necessarily. And it helped to have had the warning from Rose, even though she didn't understand it at the time. But she knew she had been on the road to caring about him—in a way that went beyond friendship. And she wondered if she'd ever find that road with anyone again.

Chapter Nine

"I hear Rose is staying with you, in your apartment." The voice was hard, bitter. If he hadn't been so congenial when he accepted her invitation to join her at her table at the William's Café as he passed by, Ginny would have waited for another time. But he was here, now, and she had the Xerox copy of the death notice in her purse, and this was eating at her. She didn't want it to go on any longer.

Tony drifted by to get Clayton Winthrop's drink order, and he was back with it swiftly, all smiles. He started to banter, but he was quick to pick up on Ginny's facial and vocal signaling that now wasn't the time—that she had something serious to talk to Winthrop about.

It had started out well enough.

"I saw the man delivering the Marie Antoinette doll to your house, Clayton. You bought it, didn't you? That was your way to insert money into Samantha's fund. You'd already done enough in other ways, you know."

Winthrop sighed and gave her a guilty little-boy look. "Yes, that was me. I just thought it would be better—for a sense of the community we have—that I not be too ostentatious about it. I can afford it."

"We do have a nice sense of community don't we, Clayton? And . . . and Rose is an important part of this community, don't you think? She called herself the queen of the square yesterday and she said it in jest. But, it's nonetheless true, isn't it?"

Clayton didn't challenge that. He didn't show any indication he agreed with it either. He just looked stubborn and took a drink from his coffee cup to hide a lack of response.

"I think we should talk about your animosity toward her." Ginny didn't know any other way to get into other than to launch into it directly.

That was when Clayton had brought up Rose sleeping in Ginny's spare room.

"Yes, I'm giving her a bed for the winter. it's cold out here after dark. I have no idea where Rose went in year's past—how she kept warm in the night during the winter. She's probably been doing it for years."

"Yes, she's been doing this little act for years. But this is the first time she has stooped to put one over on somebody like this. Do you really want to know where Rose has been going at night?"

"Yes, if you want to get into the discussion this way. But please lower your voice, Clayton. She's out there on her bench. Any louder and she'll be in the discussion with us. I know why you feel the way you do. But I know something you need to—"

"She's won you over, hasn't she? She's completely fooled you."

"Clayton, I—"

"You know who bought the Marie Antoinette doll—you ferreted that out on your own. Aren't you the least bit curious who bought the Paula Deen doll? Who paid $15,000 for that doll?"

"Yes, of course, but we were discussing—"

"That's exactly what we're discussing here, Ginny. Rose bought that doll."

"Rose?"

"Yes, and you can go see it yourself. It's sitting on the mantel in the dining room at the Armstrong Inn. It's right there for anyone and everyone to see. And do you know why it's there, Ginny?"

"No, I—" He was moving too fast for her. Slamming her left and right with new, shocking claims. But he wasn't slowing up for her. He had his head of steam. He just kept on rolling away.

"It's in the Armstrong Inn, because Rose owns that too. Why do you think it was so easy for her to get them to do a benefit for Samantha? She calls the tune there. And speaking of tune, she owns other things too—nightclubs mostly. Up and down the East Coast and in New Orleans too."

That last bit certainly hit Ginny square in the ears. Nightclubs in New Orleans. No wonder Rose could be so calm and collected about where Rodney Johnson was and whether he'd succeed in his dream of bringing money home for

Samantha's operation—and that he'd get home in time for the operation. Rose had been working on this far longer than any of the rest of them had been.

Somehow that didn't work in Rose's disfavor in Ginny's mind just now. In fact, it gave her strength, and she only let Clayton bludgeon her for one more round of this.

"And as far as needing a place to stay at night, who do you think owns that big mansion on the east side of the square, the one directly across from my place? Rose came out and sat in the park because she wanted to. She dressed like a vagrant because she wanted to. She has that big house to go home to every night. That's where she slept at night—not on the street. She's playing you. Just like she played me."

"Here, Clayton. No more. None of that makes any difference here. That's not what's eating at you. I know it's not. Here, read this. This is at the center of it all. And it's not all Rose's fault. It's not your fault either, but you need to read this."

"Read what? What's this?"

"Open it. Read it. It's only a Xerox. But I've seen the original. Rose didn't run off with your best friend while you were in Vietnam. Rose thought you were dead. And so did your best friend. They ran *to* each other for comfort—because of what they both felt for you."

"What? What are you saying?" But Ginny wouldn't say any more. She just forced him to look at the sheet of paper.

And then he read. And then he cried out in anguish. "I don't understand. This is a lie. I'm not—"

"No, you're not dead, of course. But you could be a little quieter. You could wake the dead." Ginny looked over into the park. She could see that Rose had seen them, but was trying not to show that she was watching. But Ginny was sure Rose knew what was going on over here. She hadn't retreated, though. She was sticking it out there on her bench—which, Ginny now realized, Rose might have actually bought and put there, which provided a whole new perspective on who had the right to sit there. Ginny took a deep breath and forged ahead.

"If Rose did anything wrong, it was in not showing this to you forty years ago. They sent this to your mother. Rose says this is what killed your mother. Receiving this. Rose didn't betray you. Her grief led her to your best friend. And then, when this was revealed to be a mistake, Rose had to decide what to do. If she'd left him and come back to you, would it have been any better? Would there be no scars? Would everything be hunky-dory? You may not agree with the choice Rose made—I'm not even sure I do. But she's the one who had to face the choice. And in her mind she took the road that caused the least damage—for all of the innocents involved."

Clayton sat there, hunched over into himself for the longest time. For a while Ginny could tell he was sobbing— probably more on the inside than on the surface. And then there was a period where he just rocked gently back and forth. But finally he spoke—without coming out of his crouch.

"She was so beautiful—and talented. And I loved her so. We were raised on this square. Both of us. Her in the house on the east side and me over on the west. It was like we were destined to be together. I was a writer—a poet. And she had the voice of an angel."

He straightened up a bit at this point and looked up into Ginny's face. His eyes were tear stained, but he had the hint of a smile on his lips. He spoke like he was back there, then. Like the memories were the present for him.

"She sang in all the nightclubs, you know. Her father bought them for her like they were candy, but she could have sung in them anyway. She was that good. And she wrote her own songs too—songs that inspired my poetry. We were two aspects of a single, blazing orb. And then we went—together—to the school for the arts. And Stephen was there. He was a painter. He was my friend first. I knew he wanted her, but he never made a move. He always accepted that it would be Rose and me.

"And then I got drafted. Stephen had a bad leg. Sort of like Samantha." Clayton stopped talking and then he laughed, a dry little laugh. "Now that I think of it, I think that's why Rose took Samantha up as a cause. Samantha was like Stephen—but she just didn't have the opportunities that Stephen had."

"I don't think any of this was easy for Rose, Clayton," Ginny said in a soft voice. "I don't think she loved you any less. She and Stephen didn't know—there was no reason they would have. They both loved you, and I'm sure that's where it started between them. You were the foundation for what they built together. I don't think Rose wanted to hurt you—when she knew the truth. She just didn't want to hurt Stephen either.

None of it was his fault. She just took the least disrupting route."

"Yes, I suppose. Yes, I can see that now."

"I don't think she wants anything from this. I don't think she even wants your forgiveness. I think she just wants you to be at peace with it—or at least more than you were by not knowing what caused it."

"How do you know what she's thinking, what she wants?"

"She knows I'm showing this letter to you, Clayton. She knows I'm talking to you about it. She just couldn't face trying to do it herself. She's out there in the park, watching us, but trying not to show that she is. I think she just wants there to be a peace over this."

Ginny had to give him credit. Although he was stubbornly fighting what he was hearing, she could tell that Winthrop was processing all of this, that it hadn't been a mistake for her to force it to come to light.

"You know . . . you know, I think your Aunt Marie tried talking to me once about this too. I'll bet she knew. But I wouldn't listen then."

"Maybe this isn't the time—and it certainly isn't anything Rose said she wanted—but I'm not sure that just being at peace is enough. I think you should consider more than that." Ginny felt maybe she was going too far. But she couldn't help herself. And she saw no real downside of not trying. "I think you should dream a bigger dream than that. Both of you. And I'll say the same to Rose. Maybe not today, but I'll say it."

"I'm too old. I think we're both too old—to start again."

"Oh, I don't believe anyone is too old to dream and to push the restart button, Clayton. But I'm not pushing anything here. I just think it's something you need to think about. And I also think maybe I should go now—that I've said enough. But if you'd like, we could talk again. When you've had a chance to absorb all of this."

"Yes, yes. I think I'd like that."

Ginny left him and went to Tony and told him enough about what had happened so that Tony would look after Clayton with sensitivity. And then she walked out into the park, to the bench where Rose sat.

"You told him, didn't you?"

"Yes, Rose, I did. And he told me about you. About that house over there and the Armstrong Inn and all those nightclubs. And your singing—and that you really did compose tunes."

"I figured he would."

"Why, Rose? Why did you say yes to my invitation?"

"I don't know—or at least I'm not sure. But I think I thought you needed the company. And I came to understand that I needed it as well. At my age I've come to realize that a home is more than just a roof over my head. I'm sorry I didn't see that while your Aunt Marie was alive. I imagine she chalked me up as her one failure."

"Fair enough. Will you be staying?"

"If you want me to. For a while. I'm enjoying the company."

"Fair enough. I—"

"There's an automobile in front of your place, Ginny. And a man—a very official looking man—and he's looking at us. Do you think you ought to—?"

The man was the lawyer who had informed Ginny she'd inherited the apartment and who had made all of the arrangements.

When Ginny reached his side, he handed her an envelope. "Here, Miss Standler," he said. "Your aunt asked me to deliver this letter to you three months after turning the apartment over to you. I've come to do that. Oh, and I think you might be interested to know that the will has now finished going through probate and that one of your neighbors here, a Samantha Johnson, was left a bequest of $10,000."

Ginny thanked the man and didn't suggest that he tarry any longer; he obviously wanted to be done with this transaction.

She climbed the steps to her shared foyer, anxious to get to her apartment and open the letter her Aunt Marie had left for her. Wanting to know if all she suspected was true—that her aunt had set all of this up for her—somehow knowing it was what she needed. And she'd even looked ahead on Samantha too.

"There's a man in your apartment," Arnie said to her as she entered the foyer. He startled her; she was so focused on the unopened letter in her hand that she hadn't been paying any attention. Arnie was as much on pins and needles as he had been when he'd delivered the quilt Rose had made to her.

"A man? In my apartment? Arnie, you shouldn't have—"

"Just go upstairs. I'll be right here if you need me. But . . . just . . . go upstairs."

Ginny nearly fainted at the open door to her apartment.

He was standing in the center of her living room, half at attention, but awkward, not seeming to know what to do with his hands or his legs even. He looked good in his National Guard uniform. All slicked up—as good as he'd looked the day he boarded the plane to fly to Iraq.

"Lenny? But the letter . . . I don't know why you've . . . please, don't."

And then he was at her side, keeping her from collapsing to the floor, helping her to the couch. Only then did he speak.

"I'm so sorry, Ginny. There was no letter. Oh, I know you got a letter. But I didn't send that. That was our crazy lieutenant. He did that to some of the other guys too. They only figured it out as we were getting ready to come home. He controlled our mail. He didn't give me your letters and he didn't send you my letters. He sent the one I hear you got instead. He's crazy. They've locked him up. That wasn't my letter. He told me what he'd written—and he laughed. He thought it was funny, even when he was caught at it. I thought you'd given up on me. When I found out, I was so angry. I've been looking for you for a week. I've been home for a week—looking for you. Oh, God, I love you. I'm so sorry, I . . . ."

Olivia Stowe

Olivia Stowe is a published author under different names and in other dimensions of fiction and nonfiction and lives quietly in a university town with an indulgent spouse and two demanding Siamese cats.

Books By Olivia Stowe

Spirit of Christmas

Chatham Square

By the Howling

Retired With Prejudice

Fiddler's Rest

www.cyberworldpublishing.com

www.ingramcontent.com/pod-product-compliance
Lightning Source LLC
Chambersburg PA
CBHW020141150626
46552CB00021B/1096